My Highland Mate

Middlemarch Gathering 1

Shelley Munro

My Highland Mate

Copyright © 2022 by Shelley Munro

Print ISBN: 978-1-99-115873-4
Digital ISBN: 978-1-99-115872-7

Editor: Evil Eye Editing

Cover: Kim Killion

Munro Press, New Zealand.

First Munro Press electronic publication July 2022

First Munro Press print publication July 2022

For the Village People: A warning.

This book is one of those dreadful romances and probably not to your taste. Move on—nothing to see here. But if, perchance, you decide to risk it, remember that this romance contains sex scenes. Explicit ones, 'cause that's how I roll. Read at your own risk.

One more thing: If you...*gasp*...enjoy this romance, Bruce has others locked in his bottom drawer. Go and see him for more of the same.

Introduction

Rejection ripped out her heart, but the reunion might kill her...

Years ago, Anita suffered a humiliating and devastating rejection from her fated mate. Her announcement at the pack dinner created waves that rippled through her life and changed her path. Now at the Highland gathering, she has come face-to-face with the horrid, dumb-arse stupid wolf.

She'd hoped the years would heal, but no. Every painful, embarrassing, and soul-destroying moment shoves her back into uncertainty and a vulnerable state. Worst of all, she still wants him with an instant craving that threatens to chop her off at the knees.

The problem: Rory's gawking at her as if he likes what he sees, and even worse, he asks for an introduction. He's looking and looking hard, but he doesn't recognize her...

Introducing the first romance in a Middlemarch Shifters spin-off series. A stubborn werewolf and an irked leopard shifter dance around their feelings at a special gathering to find fated mates. Forbidden love and second chances bring suspense and danger, and the handsome and oh, so sexy wolf faces up to the truth about his headstrong feline lover.

Chapter 1

Ghost From The Past

"My God, it's an honest-to-goodness castle," Suzie said as the van that had picked them up from Edinburgh airport pulled through a stone portico and into the courtyard beyond.

Anita Gatto gaped as much as her friends and fellow feline shifters from Middlemarch, New Zealand. The castle before them was a storybook one with turrets and gray stone walls. Set among a forest of pine trees, and was that a loch in the foreground? She half expected something magical to happen.

Then Anita shook herself. *Not possible.*

The six of them were here to represent their town at the biennial Highland gathering where shifters of Scottish descent came from around the world, hoping to discover their fated mate.

Not that Anita believed in the concept of a soul mate. Not any longer. Popular culture pushed the idea of fated mates, but she doubted this would happen for her.

Been there and barely escaped with her sanity.

Despite what the Middlemarch Feline Council members had informed them, Anita believed a sensible arrangement between consenting parties with common interests was way better than this mate business. But when Saber Mitchell had approached her to represent Middlemarch at the gathering, she'd agreed. Loneliness assailed her, and while a rejection from the man she'd called her mate had scarred her, she'd acquiesced to Saber's proposal because she hoped to find a like-minded shifter. If that failed, she'd at least enjoy a holiday in the Highlands.

"Well," Edwina, the third female member of their party, said. "The man with the clipboard means business. We'd better gather our enthusiasm and get this party started."

Anita exited the van and gave her name to the officious gray-haired man in a kilt. The tall, spare Scot oozed efficiency while his piercing blue eyes took in every detail. He checked her name off his list, and she waited while the others reported in with him. A shifter, but his scent baffled her, and she didn't like to question him.

The man introduced himself. "I am Angus Falconer, the castle steward. If you require anything, contact me, and I will help. Right, follow me, and I'll show you to your rooms. Someone will deliver your luggage shortly."

The castle entranceway was vast and airy, with high windows. The window facing the doorway had stained glass, and rainbows reflected and colored the whitewashed walls. On one wall, shiny silver swords displayed in a circular pattern grabbed Anita's attention, every blade large enough to lop off heads. Edwina and Suzie trailed Angus while the guys—Ramsay, Scott, and Liam—exclaimed over the weapons. Anita, who was at the rear, trotted past a suit of armor and gave it a side-eye. The armor remained frozen in position, but she sniffed the air to make sure nothing lurked inside the manlike figure.

Angus led them up stone stairs and along carpeted passages. They passed a roped-off stairway and a notice stating *Private*. One by one, her friends disappeared into their allocated rooms until only Anita remained.

"You will share with another woman. She hasn't checked in yet." The steward halted in front of a wooden door and handed over a key.

"Have most of the attendees arrived?" Anita asked.

"Aye. It's quiet now since a few have walked into town while others joined an organized fishing trip. The rest are in their rooms and preparing for the welcome ball this evening. Dinner begins at seven, and everyone is meeting in the Great Hall for pre-dinner drinks at six-thirty. You will find the relevant details and activities on the program in your room."

"Thank you," Anita said.

The steward strode away, his red and black tartan swishing around his skinny legs.

Anita sighed and pushed open her door. She wasn't looking forward to this evening. Her Middlemarch contingent had discussed the schedule, and they were of an accord. Days full of embarrassing meetings and rejections. That they might find their fated mates during a week of events was ludicrous.

Her room was beautiful and far more comfortable than she'd imagined. She even had an en suite. Small but perfectly functional, with luxurious towels and other amenities. Her explorations led her to the bank of windows. The loch view and the vibrant green of the forest beyond brightened Anita's mood. At least she'd run with other shifters this week since the castle sat on almost twenty thousand acres of mountains and pasture. Plenty of room to run and experience freedom. Heck, she could always go feline for the week.

Something to consider.

She yawned and considered a pre-dinner nap, and she'd send her snooty stepchildren a photo of the castle and perhaps some shots of the interior. *Oh, she was terrible.* Despite her arranged marriage, she'd grown fond of David and had missed him after his unexpected death even though their relationship had been tense at the end. Grinning, Anita stripped off her clothes and crawled into bed. The twenty-hour flight had exhausted her, and even though they'd stopped over in Dubai, fatigue weighted her limbs and stung her eyes. Probably the reason her mind had drifted to the past and rejection. The locale didn't help.

Scotland was her birth country, and she'd traveled to New Zealand with her much older husband and new stepchildren. Being here brought back more memories. And nope. She wasn't dwelling on the past.

Anita slept for almost three hours until her roommate, a wolf shifter from Canada, arrived.

"Sorry! I didn't mean to wake you," the redhead woman said.

Anita smiled. "I'm glad you did. It's time to shower and think about getting ready for tonight. Have you attended a gathering before?"

"No, but my older sister has. She met a bear shifter, and it was instalove. My name is Rebecca. Becky for short."

"Anita. They were fated mates?" Anita asked.

"I know. Go figure, eh? My sister adores her mate. She has two cubs and another on the way."

Anita shook her head. "Must be a fluke. I don't believe in this destined mate business."

"I hear you, but my parents nagged me to attend the gathering, so I caved. You take the first shower." Becky glanced at her watch. "Better make it fast because it's five-thirty. It pays to get to the Great Hall early. Soak in the details and inform people back home you're meeting lots of shifters."

"Brilliant plan, Becky. We're gonna get along fine."

Three-quarters of an hour later, Anita ascended the stairs with Becky. The Great Hall was already bustling with attendees. Most of the men wore kilts, and Anita, like the other women, wore a plain dress trimmed with the gray, green, and blue Middlemarch tartan that the Feline Council had ordered before their departure. A mixture of perfume and aftershave swirled together, along with the meaty scent wafting from the roving waitstaff's trays.

Anita glanced around the crowded room, listening to the chatter and laughter, the flirtation that was already going strong between shifter men and women.

"Let's get a drink. Ah, here comes one of the waiter dudes." Becky plucked two glasses of champagne off the tray, leaving the waiter scowling.

Anita sent the man a sympathetic smile since she'd worked as waitstaff at several functions in Dunedin. The worst thing you could do was snatch the drinks off a tray because the balance was tricky.

She trailed Becky through the crowded room, stopping when she spotted Ramsay, Liam, and Scott, the male members of the Middlemarch party. Anita slowed, intending to introduce her roomie, but Becky disappeared into the crowd.

"This feels like a meat market," Scott whispered, his tanned face scrunched in a scowl.

Ramsay chuckled, his black hair tamed in a tail for this event. "You're out of sorts because you didn't want to wear the Middlemarch kilt."

"Why don't I take a photo of us and email it to Saber? He'll share it with the council members, and they'll know we've started the right way," Anita said.

"Plan," Liam said, his blue-green eyes filling with amusement.

They crowded closer, shoulders touching, and Anita held up her phone to snap the shot. "Done. Let me take one of the three of you together so that they can *ooh* and *ah* over your kilts."

"You just want to see our legs," Scott complained, raising his kilt to display most of his muscular limbs.

"And very nice legs they are too," Anita said, trying not to laugh. She took the photo and was about to ask Ramsay to take one of her when a fresh scent claimed her attention. It was the fragrance of Scotland—heather and sage and a hint of pine rolled together with wood smoke. She froze before dragging in one careful lungful of air.

"What's wrong?" Ramsay's green eyes narrowed. "You've turned the color of a batch of meringues."

Ramsay was a chef, so the food comparison made sense, but what didn't fit was the enticing scent and her reaction to it. She took two steps toward the decadent piney herbal musk, her gaze wandering the sea of faces. Her mouth turned dry, and her stomach churned because the fragrance brought back memories—embarrassing ones.

No, this couldn't be. It was Anita's imagination conjuring reminders because she'd returned to Scotland, the scene of her downfall. Anita swallowed hard, but this did nothing to shift the dryness of her throat. She sipped her crisp, fruity champagne and then drank more until no liquid remained. *Better.*

Once again, Anita scanned the faces of myriad shifters around her, all enjoying the drinks, snacks, and company. She sniffed carefully, her gaze landing on the nearest couple. The sweet berry musk of a bear. A hint of honey. Also, a bear. They had eyes only for each other. She continued, making a game of identifying the shifters.

"What's wrong, Anita?" Ramsay pitched his voice low, but she heard his distinct worry.

"I caught a whiff of a familiar scent—one that doesn't come with glorious memories." Honesty as far as it went.

"Are you in danger?"

"No. At least I don't think so." Anita forced a laugh. "I'm sure I'm imagining things. It's being back in Scotland."

"All right." He didn't seem convinced, but he backed off. "I feel as if everyone is looking at me. The women," he amended.

Anita smiled, the curve of her lips more natural now. "Ramsay, you're an attractive man, and you don't come with oodles of attitude and swagger.

11

You're friendly. Any woman would be lucky to win your love."

"I don't come from a wonderful family."

Anita snorted. "The Mitchells have adopted you. They're good people and excellent judges of character. You have nothing to worry about."

A movement to her right caught her attention, and she glanced in that direction. The crowd was thick, with more attendees appearing by the minute. Becky had been right to suggest they arrive early.

Then that wretched scent floated to her again. The champagne tap-danced in the pit of her stomach, and she struggled to hold it down. She swallowed once. Twice.

This scent. It was familiar and one that lingered in her nightmares. A shudder worked through her, and Anita attempted to find the source of the smell.

Movement at the door had her turning. The distinct sound of bagpipes inflating sounded an instant before a lone piper marched into the Great Hall. The crowd split for the piper, allowing passage to the dining room beyond.

It was then Anita spotted him.

Rory Henderson.

The wolf who'd rejected her, even though Anita had been confident they were mates.

Her champagne flute dropped from nerveless fingers as she stared at her past. The thud of glass breaking attracted attention. *His attention.* His gaze swung in Anita's direction.

Anita turned away to shield her face and pressed a hand to her breastbone. She dragged in a shaky breath, her mind whirring. As far as she knew, Rory Henderson had married another wolf. Her parents had told her this, and Anita had no reason not to believe them.

But if that was true, why was Rory Henderson at a singles' gathering?

Chapter 2

Challenge Accepted

Rory Henderson heard the hubbub of chatter long before he reached the Great Hall. A hint of roast beef drifted from a kitchen, tucked somewhere close but out of sight. That delicious dinner aroma faded under the onslaught of perfume and aftershave. His wolf senses picked up a shifter musk—many shifters of varying species. He wrinkled his nose, sneezed, and breathed through his mouth.

This was why he preferred to stay at home in the mountains, surrounded by pines, birch, and the odd oak. He favored the crisp mountain air and hard work to ascertain his pack not only survived but thrived.

His grandmother thought otherwise and continually nagged him to take a female wolf and produce the next generation. She wanted him to choose her friend's granddaughter. Rory disliked her candidate, and attending the biennial Highland gathering was the compromise.

The truth was even though he loved his mountain life and producing the quality furniture his pack had become known for designing, he was lonely.

Not a substantial reason to take his grandmother's candidate to wife.

"Let's do this," he said to his male pack mates. They were here to act as bodyguards, but he didn't need security. This was another of his grandmother's conditions. Her spies, he suspected but didn't care. As long as he joined the gathering activities, everything would work fine.

Rory paused on the threshold, taking in the room's occupants. Most, like him, wore their clan tartans since every shifter bore Scottish ties.

The power of a stare hit his chest, and every muscle in his body tightened like a compressed spring. Casually, he spoke to the werewolf on his left. "Do you see anyone you know?" He let his gaze sweep their surroundings as he spoke. Like a magnet, his attention focused on the staring woman.

A stranger and an attractive one. She had long black hair and skin the color of honey. He couldn't see her eyes, but he was the object of her interest.

"Nope," his security guard said. "But I see lots of sexy ladies who I wouldn't mind becoming acquainted with before the week ends."

Rory waved his hand. "Have at it. Don't stay by my side. If you find someone interesting, follow your instincts."

The men hesitated.

"The only danger here is single shifters searching for a mate. I'm old enough and wise enough to cope with the ladies. I don't intend to make mistakes or let any female drag me into a situation where she forces me to make her my wife."

"If you're positive," one wolf said.

"That's an order," Rory said. "Go. I have my phone and will call if I need you."

By the time his security team had vanished, Rory couldn't spot the woman. A waiter passed and offered Rory a glass of champagne.

"Is it possible to have a beer?"

"Yes, sir. Check the bar in the far corner. They'll get you a beer."

"Thanks." Rory walked in the direction the waiter had indicated, dodging groups and inattentive shifters. He felt the crawl of gazes, flicking the length of his body and mentally undressing him. *Bloody hell.* Putting up with this for the entire week would strain his temper. He fervently wished he hadn't given in to his grandmother's urging for him to take a wife.

He didn't see the woman again, although he searched for her.

The piper who'd arrived before him finished his bagpipe rendition. An older man wearing a kilt announced dinner. "Please check in with the hostesses just inside the door."

The piper started a rousing 'Scotland the Brave' before leading the crowd into dinner.

Rory waited until the crowd thinned before heading to the dining room. The delectable roast beef scent was even heavier in the air, and his stomach rumbled. At least the food stirred his appetite. That was a plus.

"Your name, sir?"

"Rory Henderson."

The woman consulted her list. "Table eleven. This way. The table toward the end of the row."

"Thanks." Rory made way for the next person in the line.

Chairs slid across the flagstone floor as diners took their seats. Old acquaintances called loud shouts of welcome, and Rory heard more than one person mention they were here for a repeat gathering since they still hadn't found a mate.

Huh! And his grandmother expected the mating lightning bug to hit him. Doubtful, and even less so given his lack of interest.

Rory shook himself from his thoughts and hustled along the line of tables until he reached table eleven. The woman he'd spied earlier already sat at the table, and he slid into the seat beside her. She took one look at him and froze, her champagne halting halfway to her mouth. She swallowed hard, and her glass trembled before she set it on the starched white tablecloth.

Rory thrust out his right hand, not liking the idea that something about his appearance startled her. "Rory Henderson. What was your name?"

Her mouth firmed, and she stared at him for a beat longer before extending her hand. "Anita Gatto."

Her fingers were soft and warm, and she withdrew them too fast for his liking. "You're not from around here. Your accent tells me that."

"I flew in with a group from New Zealand," she said, watching him closely.

He cocked his head. "Do I know you?"

She scowled and turned her attention to the hovering waitress without answering him.

"Are you ready to order?" the young woman asked.

"Yes, of course." Anita picked up her menu before decisively choosing a pate starter and roast beef for her main.

The waitress took Anita's menu and turned to him. "What would you like, sir?"

"The potted smoked salmon and the roast beef, please," Rory said.

The waitress claimed his menu and moved on to the next person.

Rory glanced at Anita. "Have you been to the gathering before?"

"No, none of our New Zealand group has attended before," Anita replied. "We're not sure what to expect."

"Me neither," Rory said. "A man from our village attended. He didn't return but traveled to Europe with a bear shifter. Or at least that's what the gossip says." His grandmother had been definite: she'd ordered him to ignore non-wolf shifters. This woman was feline. "Where in New Zealand? North or South Island?"

"We're from the South Island—a small country town close to Dunedin."

Rory noticed she didn't inquire where he lived. In fact, she wasn't adding to the conversation at all, merely answering his questions abruptly, her voice clipped and disinterested.

"Are you here under protest?"

"No."

"So it's me you don't want to speak with?"

"Yes."

"Why?"

"I have my reasons."

"But we don't know each other." He scrutinized her and noted the slight flinch.

"How could we? I live in New Zealand."

The woman sitting on his other side claimed his attention. A subtle sniff told Rory the curvy woman was a bear. She winked at him.

"Not interested in a mixed mating?" she asked.

"It wouldn't go down well with my pack."

She shrugged. "What happens at the gathering stays at the gathering. This is my third time. My stepmother is determined to get rid of me. She's hoping the third time is the charm."

"And what do you think?" Rory asked.

"The gathering should be fun, but the local human mechanic near my work has my heart. I'll wear down my father soon if I can annoy my stepmother enough to get over her snobbery."

Rory chuckled. "You have a plan."

"What I have is a *winning* plan."

"Confidence is half the battle," the guy sitting on the female shifter's other side said.

Rory let their conversation drift over him while surreptitiously watching Anita. The woman's honey-colored skin seemed paler than earlier, and she gripped her cutlery like weapons. Now and then, she'd sneak a glance at him. Her scowl told Rory something about him upset her.

Rory thought he was an easygoing guy. He was happiest sorting out problems diplomatically rather than knocking heads together. Hell, he couldn't think of anything he might've done to upset this feline woman. Rory seldom left the mountain where he lived and worked.

A brainwave occurred to Rory. "Have you visited Scotland before?"

Her brown eyes widened, and she shook her head vigorously. "This is my first visit."

She averted her gaze before letting it skitter back. Finally, she glanced down at her silverware.

Rory grimaced, glad when a waiter interrupted to take their drink orders.

"We have red or white table wine. Which would you prefer?" the waiter asked.

The female bear shifter butted into the conversation. "We'll have one of each," she chirped.

The waiter smiled and handed over two bottles of wine.

"White or red?" Something about Anita made Rory want to annoy her, to force her to speak to him. He didn't take the time to analyze his reaction but tilted the white in her direction. "You do want wine?"

"Please," she said, her voice harsh.

Rory inhaled, and her floral scent filled his nostrils. Nice. Her perfume was delicate instead of overpowering, and something about the smell poked at his memories. He shook himself and tamped down his uneasy wolf.

Once he'd filled her glass, she lifted it to her red lips and took a huge sip. Rory turned to his right to offer the white wine. When he turned back, her glass was empty.

Rory topped up her glass. "Do I make you nervous?"

"No!"

"Are you interested in me?"

"No." Her feline showed in her golden-brown eyes. An intriguing but fleeting flash of temper lit her features. "You're a wolf."

"Mixed marriages are common these days." Not in his world, but he wanted to rile her and provoke a reaction.

She bit her lip and didn't reply to his statement, although he could tell she wanted to snap at him because her jaw clenched. Her feline was practically spitting at him, and if she were in her feline form, she'd take a swipe at him with unleashed claws.

"We could partner in the activities." Rory didn't stop to analyze his impulse to needle her to get a reaction.

"I don't think so," came her chilly reply.

Interesting. Anita's accent held the distinct sounds of her home country, but beneath, he caught a hint of the Scottish brogue. No, perhaps he imagined this, or maybe... "Were your parents born in Scotland?"

"None of your business." She drank more of her wine and ignored him to chat with the man on her other side.

Rory tapped her on the shoulder, his inner wolf irritated at the casual way she'd dismissed him.

"Leave me alone. Wolves don't interest me."

"Right." Rory shaped his mouth into a toothy grin. "Challenge accepted."

Chapter 3

This Is Not Happening

Every muscle in Anita's body locked. She elbowed the aberrant yearning away and locked it in a mental safe. She added an internal danger sign and wrapped a chain around the closure. That should do the trick.

This wolf was not for her.

He'd rejected her when she was eighteen years old. His grandmother had confirmed Rory and she would never be lovers, never become partners.

Never. Never. *Never.*

The ugly scenes burst to life like ignited fireworks, flickering in fast-moving pictures through her mind. She recalled the embarrassment, the silence in a Great Hall much like this one. She could still remember the stares and sneering laughter. The ridicule that came from Rory's pack because she—a feline shifter with the physique of a child—had dared to claim the heir apparent as her mate.

Did fate hate her this much?

Before the gathering had even formally started, destiny had tossed her in Rory Henderson's path, seating her right beside him for dinner.

Talk about unlucky.

Her right hand trembled noticeably when she reached for her wineglass. The despicable memories kept repeating like a horror movie on constant replay. She'd been so young back then and full of confidence. So convinced that announcing Rory was her destined mate would click everything into place.

Of course, her grand plan had derailed almost straightaway.

As well as being a late bloomer, she'd possessed terrible skin thanks to her chocolate and sweet habit. Homemade sweets had been her biggest vice, and she'd loved to create variations of classic fudge recipes.

Anita's behavior had appalled Rory's grandmother, and two senior bodyguards had escorted her back to the house on Henderson Castle grounds where she and her parents lived. The house came with her father's gamekeeper job. The bodyguards had locked Anita in her bedroom, and Rory's grandmother had summoned Anita's father to the castle.

A week later, she'd been en route to New Zealand and married to an older man, a widower with two girls. She hadn't expected to encounter Rory on this first visit to Scotland.

She'd decided a spot in Saber Mitchell's group to attend the gathering held little risk. Anita had agreed because her life had become routine and stagnant, and lately, she'd thought about having children. She'd seen Saber's suggestion as a sign.

A delusion, she realized now. She gulped more wine and coughed when it went down the wrong way.

Rory cocked his head. "Shouldn't you drink a little slower? We haven't had dinner yet. If you keep gulping alcohol like that, you'll end up drunk."

Anita winged a glare in Rory's direction without catching his eye. He had no right to her obedience. He'd lost that power the instant he'd refuted her mate claim.

"Here, have some water."

The temptation to toss the liquid in his handsome face almost overwhelmed her. The years had treated him well. His dark brown hair held a red tint that grew more evident during the height of summer, and his blue eyes reminded her of a Scottish loch on a cloudless, sunny day. Five years older than her, he'd grown into his lanky limbs, and his golden skin told her he spent time outdoors.

Rory set the glass of water down, and a silent warning blared through her on seeing the interest, the speculation in those lake-blue eyes.

Interest was the last thing she needed.

"What do you want of me? You're a wolf, and I'm a feline. I am not interested in an inter-species marriage." Her lips pressed together, and since Rory seemed disinclined to refill her wineglass, she asked the man sitting beside her if he could pass her a bottle.

He did and offered her a charming smile while he topped up her glass.

"Thank you." Her smile grew more genuine, even though he was a wolf, too.

Rory's grandmother had set out strict conditions when she'd spoken to Anita's father. She expect-ed her grandson to mate with another wolf. There would be no bloodline mixing in their pack.

Another thought occurred, and pique struck like lightning, leaving her stunned once she saw the truth of this idea. *Rory didn't recognize her.* While she'd changed radically in appearance, he hadn't blinked on hearing her name. His current smile was one suitable for a new acquaintance. Friendly. Open. Slightly flirtatious.

His regard churned her stomach, but her feline basked under the attention. *Silly cat.* Rory Henderson would *not* stomp over their feelings again.

"Are you ignoring me?" The low voice held a trace of amusement.

Okay. Snubbing Rory wasn't working. Time to suck it up and converse with him like an adult. Once this dinner ended, she'd avoid his company. She'd speak with the organizers and request no matches or face time with Rory Henderson. Edwina or Suzie, the other two Middlemarch women, would swap with her if necessary. Yeah, that'd work.

She slid him a side-eye. "I had nothing to say, so I remained quiet."

His blue eyes twinkled. "Ah, a woman who doesn't chatter for the sake of filling a silence. My favorite kind."

Anita sipped her wine, pushing herself to take her time and savor the fruity notes instead of slugging it back. Hopefully, their appetizers would arrive soon, so she had food to help settle her stomach.

"Your accent. Australian?" the wolf shifter sitting on her left asked.

"I'm from New Zealand. You?"

"I came over from Canada with a group from my pack. I'm Richard."

"Anita. Are you looking for a mate?"

"If someone tempts me, I wouldn't say no, but I'm not ready to settle down with one woman."

"An honest man." Anita glanced upward. "Has the sky fallen?"

Richard laughed, a huge booming sound that attracted attention from the neighboring tables. "My parents decided this'd be a life-building experience. Um, I might've been getting into a little trouble with my friends."

Anita studied the blond man and noted he was younger than her first guess. Too immature for her.

A line of waitresses entered the Great Hall, each carrying appetizers. Anita relaxed and introduced herself to those seated at the same table. Most of the shifters she'd met so far were feline, wolf, or bear, but she'd met two fox shifters.

A waitress placed pate in front of Anita. She smiled her thanks and chatted with Richard while waiting for everyone to receive their appetizers. Then she glanced down at her plate. The scent tossed her deep into memories of when she was eighteen and approaching Rory Henderson to declare she was his mate.

A fine film of perspiration coated her skin, and a croaking sound escaped her. Her limbs became heavy weights, anchoring her in place, and the scene—the awful, horrid tableau—kept replaying on a loop. She recalled the shock on Rory's face, his parents' contempt, and the disgust written on his grandmother's chilly visage.

She'd stood, frozen, unprepared for Rory's grandmother to issue the order to two warrior guards to remove her from the Great Hall.

Anita sucked in a hasty breath to ease the tension crawling through her limbs. She was no longer that young feline girl with a head full of dreams. She'd married and helped to raise stepchildren. And after her husband had passed, she'd made a home for herself. She had friends in Middlemarch, a respectable life, even if loneliness blitzed her at times.

Another deep breath seized the meaty liver pate scent and grabbed at her throat. Her stomach lurched, and she gulped.

Oh, hell.

She was gonna be sick.

She had to get out of here. Anita pushed back her chair and knocked into a waitress carrying a tray. Plates crashed to the floor. Conversations stalled. Shifters at other tables turned to stare. Rory stood and squatted to help the waitress pick up the broken pieces of china.

"I'm sorry." Anita gasped, her stomach bucking and roiling. She took two steps past the mess of plates and food, mostly pate, she noted. The liver-rich scent rose, and Anita lost the fight. She barfed all over Rory Henderson.

The ugly scent of vomit joined that of the pate. Anita's throat burned as another wave of nausea had her repeating the act.

"I'm so sorry," she managed before she clapped her hand over her mouth and fled.

Chapter 4

Mine

Rory gaped after the fleeing woman before glancing down at his favorite kilt. This was a first. No woman had ever vomited over him before.

He turned his attention to the flustered waitress. "Are you all right, lass?"

"Aye, of course. The lady didn't mean to knock into me. It's obvious she isn't feeling well." She grimaced. "Nothing contagious, I hope."

"Me too," he said instead of divulging his true thoughts. He'd somehow upset the woman, as she'd behaved like a prickly hedgehog from the moment they'd met.

A waiter appeared with a brush and pan.

"Thank you, sir," he said firmly. "I'll take over. You'll be wanting to change before you eat."

"Aye. Thank you."

One of his men appeared, his brow creased in concern, but Rory waved him away. "I'll go to my room and be back in ten minutes."

His man glanced at his kilt and wrinkled his nose. "No offense, boss, but you honk."

Rory rolled his eyes. "Thank you, Captain Obvious. Won't be long."

"If you're not back within half an hour, we'll come looking for you."

Rory offered a clipped nod and strode from the Great Hall before he snapped something he shouldn't. His grandmother's orders, no doubt. Of an older generation, Elizabeth was determined to choose a suitable female wolf for him.

Usually, he nodded and agreed with his grandmother, then did his own thing. Even though Elizabeth pretended she still ruled the pack, he was the alpha. They butted heads often, although no one ever witnessed these *discussions*.

Rory tried not to resent her interference and determination to adhere to the old ways. His thoughts waltzed back to the feline shifter. She intrigued him, and he wanted to get acquainted. He needed to understand her reasons for pushing him away and was desperate to learn what he'd done to upset her so he could set about fixing his misstep.

But, to appease his grandmother, tonight he'd circulate after dinner and speak to other shifter women. His grandmother would've ordered his security detail to keep her informed.

Rory swore as he strode up the curving stairs that led to the next floor and his chamber. His grandmother must cease this interference, but the best way to assert his authority eluded him. How did he show her that although she was family and he loved her, she couldn't revoke his orders or direct his behavior? He'd decide on his mate, and he didn't care if it was a wolf, a bear, a feline, or another type of shifter.

Rory's mate shopping list included decency, a woman he found attractive and genuinely liked, someone who preferred living in an isolated region, and a shifter who wanted children. He wanted a partner to stand at his side.

A friend. A best friend.

So far, his grandmother's candidates had lacked most or all of these attributes.

He added loyalty to him to his list and made a promise to himself that on his return to Castle Henderson, he'd set his grandmother straight and tell her to butt out.

On the way to his room, his wolf stirred, standing to attention. A growl worked up his throat, sounding loud in the silent hallway. Rory glanced left and right but saw nothing to provoke this behavior.

Mine. Mine. Mine.

The words chanted through his brain, his wolf agitated.

Rory slowed and inhaled. He cast out his senses and analyzed the distinct scents. Hints of wolf, bear, and feline tickled his nostrils.

His wolf growled again. Feline. Rory stiffened because, along with the cat scent, came the distinct odor of vomit.

Anita?

His wolf wanted Anita.

Rory grinned. Now that made sense because the standoffish woman had snared his interest from the instant he'd spotted her. He and his wolf agreed, which made life a lot easier.

He followed the scent until it ended at a doorway halfway down the passage. Rory halted, hesitating. No, he'd leave Anita alone tonight and use the time apart to form a strategy. The glimpse he'd caught of her seconds before she fled had been of pink cheeks. People had stared, and he'd gained the impression she was a private, guarded person.

Aye, he'd let her regain her confidence, and tomorrow, he'd unleash his charm.

The following day, Rory awakened with a spring in his step. Last night, he'd returned to dinner and participated in the dancing afterward. Anita hadn't returned, but her absence pleased him and his wolf since it meant the other males remained at a distance.

Breakfast was a casual affair, but most people were up and heaping their plates with bacon and eggs and pancakes. Planned activities for the day included a scavenger hunt, a dating game quiz, and an afternoon tea mixer. Those who preferred physical exercise headed for the organized strength and cunning activities the Scottish excelled at playing.

The whispers that crept through the dining hall were Rory's first clues of Anita's presence. She marched into the room with her head held high and surrounded by a group of feline shifters.

Admiration filled Rory. That took guts since he'd heard the gossip and joking laughter about how the shifter men should stay away since she'd vomit on them. She didn't look sick this morning, so he figured a combination of fatigue, lack of food, and too much alcohol had caused her illness.

Although his wolf urged him to approach and cut her from her clan, Rory resisted. He'd hang back and attempt to eavesdrop on the conversation to get an idea of what activity she and her friends would choose to fill their morning.

Luckily, Anita's group picked a table near where he sat, eating his morning porridge. They were far enough away to make Anita comfortable and close enough for him to use his wolfish hearing to listen in to their conversations.

"Anyone met anyone interesting yet?" a woman asked, her accent more pronounced than Anita's.

"I don't want to make a hasty decision," a man said.

"Yeah, I'm with Ramsay. Saber told us to meet other shifters and have fun," a different woman said. "That's what I intend to do, no matter what my grandmother expects."

Anita snorted. "Your grandmothers should've learned by now that you'll do what you want and not follow orders."

"Slow learners," the woman replied, and the entire group guffawed.

"What are you doing this morning, Anita?" one man asked.

"The scavenger hunt sounds like fun, and it will be nice to explore the gardens."

"The prize is enticing," a blonde woman said. "Who wouldn't want a holiday on a tropical island?"

Good point. Rory didn't find it challenging to imagine Anita in a tiny bikini or nothing at all. He grinned down at his almost empty plate. A tropical holiday would be the perfect place to take his mate on their honeymoon.

As soon as he thought about it, he froze. His mate? While it was true, he found her intriguing, he didn't believe in the special mate destined for him. That was pure fiction, yet he couldn't refute the attraction and the way the aloof woman was filling his thoughts.

A feline shifter.

Not a problem for him, but his grandmother's reaction... She'd have kittens.

Early days. Hiding his grin, Rory rose from the breakfast table and sauntered from the dining hall without glancing at Anita. However, he was insanely aware of her, and her scent flooded each of his breaths—an earthy fragrance, resplendent with floral notes. It was his new favorite. He had to force himself to keep moving. He'd head off for a walk to regain his control before he turned up for the scavenger hunt.

Who he ended up with on his team was out of his control, but maybe fate would land on his side?

Chapter 5

The Gathering Begins

"He's cute," Suzie said, staring after the man Anita was trying to ignore and avoid. The blasted wolf kept popping into her location like a magical genie.

Edwina laughed. "That's the shifter Anita barfed on. He's frightened to come too close in case she does a repeat performance."

"Haha," Anita muttered. "Hilarious. Is anyone interested in a walk?"

"I'm up for one." Ramsay checked his watch. "We have time before the day's activities begin."

Anita lingered over her coffee, waiting until Rory disappeared, before swallowing the dregs and standing. "I'm ready."

Ramsay stood, and they left the castle together.

"We can stroll around the loch. The sign says it takes less than an hour," Ramsay said.

They wandered into the forest, the temperature cooler than out in the open. The fresh pine filled Anita's lungs, and the tenseness faded from her muscles. The gathering would be enjoyable if it weren't for Rory's presence. Meeting new people always invigorated her, and the fact one hundred percent were shifters made this an incredible opportunity.

"Are you feeling better?" Ramsay asked.

"Yes, thanks. I'm not sure what happened. Maybe a mix of nerves, alcohol on an empty stomach and—"

"Anita." Ramsay folded his arms over his chest, his green eyes full of patience and humor and friendship. His black hair lifted in the faint breeze. "You have a cast-iron stomach and handle alcohol better than me. What's going on? You were fine until that guy sat beside you, then you fell to pieces."

Anita closed her eyes and heaved out a loud sigh. When she opened her eyes again, Ramsay regarded her with a lopsided grin. "Why hasn't a smart woman snapped you up?"

"I'm a busy man. Work leaves little time for socializing. I wanted to excel in my studies and the practical side of cooking."

"Seen anyone to tempt you here?"

"You're changing the subject." Ramsay grabbed her hand and dragged her along the path. "Walk and talk."

Anita sighed again. "My parents worked for Rory's grandmother."

"He didn't recognize you. I mean, he was interested, but he treated you like a new acquaintance."

"I'm not the same scrawny eighteen-year-old who informed him he was my mate."

"He rejected you?" Ramsay grasped the gist of her story without her needing to paint the details.

"Yeah. I wasn't an attractive teen. Back then, I was a scrawny feline. Rory's grandmother wanted to keep the pack pure. She wants wolf great-grandchildren with not a hint of any other shifter. My father lost his job because of my actions."

"Hell," Ramsay said as they exited the pines and got a clear view of the loch. "Where did your family go? What happened?"

"My father took a job at an English estate."

"I hear a but at the end of that sentence."

She exhaled a gusty breath. "My parents decided they couldn't trust me not to cause more chaos in their lives. They arranged a marriage for me with an older man with two children."

"But you were eighteen."

"Didn't matter. I was of age. My new husband had decided to emigrate to New Zealand for a fresh start since Scotland held too many memories of his wife. He'd loved her, but he needed help with the children. That was my job."

"It was a marriage of convenience?"

"Convenient for him. He got a babysitter, bed partner, and maid in one sweep."

Ramsay scowled. "Did he mistreat you?"

Anita shrugged. "No, not really. We didn't have a passionate marriage, but we became friends. I miss him."

"How long have you been a widow?"

"Almost three years now."

"What about your stepchildren?"

"They don't like me." Anita lengthened her strides, trying to outrun the truth and the questions. She never discussed this because it made her remember the failure of her marriage. Toward the end, they'd argued more, and she'd suspected David was having an affair. There had been something fishy about his death in the Wellington hotel room. Her oldest stepdaughter had taken care of the formalities since she worked in the capital, too.

"How old are your stepchildren now?" Ramsay persisted.

"Irene is around your age. She's twenty-five, and Susan is twenty-two."

"They're not much younger than you. You're what, thirty-two?

"Thirty-one," Anita said. "Do you think we'll make it back for the start of the scavenger hunt?"

Ramsay curved his fingers around her shoulder. "Stop changing the subject. I told you about my background during the flight. Fair's fair. Have your stepdaughters always been difficult?"

"They resented their father for replacing their mother so fast. After David died, they disagreed about his will and money. They had their mother's jewelry and the apartment in Wellington, and we each had equal shares in the house in Christchurch."

"What happened?"

"We sold the house and split the proceeds three ways. I haven't spoken to the girls since. As far as they're concerned, we're not related, and they don't owe me a damn thing."

"That must be difficult when you nurtured them for all those years."

"Honestly, they made my life hell, but never in front of David. I tried not to let it show, but it was a happy day when David decided the girls should attend a boarding school in Auckland and spend time with their mother's sister during the holidays. David flew up to visit them every few months, but I'd started an office management job to fill my days by that time. I couldn't get time off as easily as David, so I stayed at home." Anita came to a standstill at the loch and studied the sweeping castle turrets. They gleamed in the morning light. "I'm glad I let you talk me into this walk. I'd missed Scotland."

"You didn't think of returning?"

"My parents wiped their hands of me from the moment I left."

"But you're here now," Ramsay said.

"Against my better judgment, I let Saber talk me into this visit. He got me at a bad time, and I caved because I was lonely and feeling sorry for myself."

Ramsay brushed shoulders with her and cast her a grin. "Huh! He pulled a similar trick on me. Got me in a weak moment."

Anita chuckled. "I tell you what. While Saber might want us to find mates, there's no reason to attend every event and activity. Did you check the evening's entertainment?"

"Another dinner and dancing afterward. They called it a mixer."

"Want to play hooky and go sightseeing later this afternoon? Instead of returning for dinner, we can have a meal at the pub. There's bound to be a decent pub in the village."

"Transport?" Ramsay asked.

"Uber," Anita said. "The village is large enough for a taxi service, but it's not far to walk."

"Plan," Ramsay said. "If you see the others, invite them to come with us."

"Edwina and Suzie were going to the scavenger hunt. The guys... No clue. I'll ask them if I see them, and you do the same."

"Deal," Ramsay said. "Now, let's try to win this tropical island holiday."

"Huh! Fat chance. I bet most shifters will try to win. The compere told us there were one hundred and fifty attendees."

Ramsay pursed his lips in a whistle. "That's a lot of single shifters. What are the chances of finding mates? I can imagine Edwina and Suzie's grandmothers jumping up and down if the Council's investment in us doesn't work."

"Saber told me this was a learning process. It was no problem if we returned still single. I asked him because I didn't want to feel beholden or suffer from stress."

"Then what's the point?"

"Saber wants us to chat with shifters and listen when they discuss how their packs cope with modern-day pressures," Anita said.

"That's why we need to report once we arrive back home."

"Yup. We'd better head back otherwise, we'll miss the start."

The crackle of dry leaves had them spinning to peer into the tangled undergrowth. A large black wolf trotted out and, unconcerned with their presence, continued down the loch path leading to the castle.

After several minutes, Ramsay said, "Did you hear the wolf coming? Smell him?"

"No," Anita said. "The breeze was blowing away from us. Do you think he was eavesdropping?"

"Why? He's probably out for a walk like us. I keep forgetting we have the freedom to shift at will here. Everyone is a shifter, so it doesn't matter if we walk on two legs or four."

Anita reached for Ramsay's hand and tugged. "Come on. One of us has to win this luxury holiday. The Feline Council could raise funds for the community by raffling it off."

Ramsay grinned and squeezed her hand. "Always thinking. I like that in a woman. It's a pity you feel more like a sister."

Anita gave him a brief hug before dancing two steps in the castle's direction. "Come on. Maybe one of us will fluke it and find our mate. Stranger things have happened."

Chapter 6

Scavenger Hunt

Rory trotted toward the castle, his mind on the woman. *Anita.* He hadn't meant to eavesdrop on their conversation, but once his wolf had caught their scent, Rory had lost control then given up. His wolf desired the dark-haired woman. He didn't care she was a feline. He didn't care his grandmother expected a she-wolf to join their pack.

No, his wolf had focused on taking the woman and marking her as theirs.

Rory hadn't heard the start of the conversation, but he'd heard them arrange to visit the local pub. His wolf growled deep in his throat, his aggravation clear. They both disliked the closeness between the pair, their easy conversation.

But what should Rory do about it?

Did he ignore his instincts and coast through the week? He could tell his grandmother not one of the shifter women had attracted his wolf's attention, which would leave him back at the start with Elizabeth's plans. She'd attempt to force her friend's daughter on him. She'd discuss ad nauseam and chip at his resolve, or at least she'd try.

Now that he'd met Anita, he refused to settle for his grandmother's candidate.

He replayed the couple's conversation in his mind. Anita had been married, and her husband had died. She had stepchildren. His grandmother wanted him to marry a virgin. While it didn't matter to him—it honestly didn't—he couldn't help the snarl of displeasure that escaped him.

Jealousy.

Neither he nor his wolf approved of her keeping company with the man who was a close friend, which meant Rory would visit that pub tonight. His security detail would tag along, but he could ditch them later.

As soon as he pried Anita from her friends, he'd start his seduction.

Three wolves joined him, but he didn't flinch because he recognized their scents. He continued his fast trot toward the castle to give himself time to change. Although he and the other contestants didn't know the rules of the scavenger hunt yet, the short blurb in the "What's On" leaflet had mentioned everyone must hunt for their clues on two legs.

The line of contestants was far longer than he'd envisioned, and he frowned. How the hell could he finagle Anita onto his team?

The compere arrived. Rory blinked. What the heck was the man wearing? His kilt sparkled in the morning light, and a disco ball came to mind. A lone piper accompanied the flamboyant man. As the last notes died, the compere held up his right hand for silence. "Please, everyone. Line up. Males in one line and females in another. Ladies, you stay in your line for now and talk amongst yourself. Gentlemen, please move forward and speak to our three lovely assistants."

Rory waited his turn. The shifters in front of him glanced at the women, and each walked the line and chose one. Rory's heart hammered when a man paused in front of Anita, then continued onward when she scowled at him.

A challenge. Rory hid his victorious grin. She didn't want a mate.

He had a tough job in front of him, but he could woo and win her affection. She was strong and mouthy and unafraid to speak her mind. That would stand her in excellent stead when coming face to face with his grandmother.

She had dark beauty, and intelligence shone in her golden-brown eyes. She dressed nicely but didn't bare too much skin. At least she hadn't last night. That wasn't a deal-breaker, but he didn't want other men ogling his mate. If she preferred to live in a town or city, that would be a problem. He couldn't imagine living cheek to jowl with humans and other shifters because he loved the beauty of the mountains and the contentment he found making his furniture.

Something to consider once he spent time with the woman.

Rory reached the head of the line.

"Name," the woman asked.

"Rory Henderson."

"You have two hours to find the items on your list. You can begin as soon as the starter fires his gun. Please choose your partner, then wait with the other teams. One point before you commence—partners must remain together. If we find you on your own, it will disqualify you."

Rory accepted the list and stalked halfway along the line until he reached Anita. He stopped in front of her, and she glared at him.

"Go away. Pick someone else," she said in a clear voice.

"I want you."

"What if I vomit on you again?"

"You look healthy. We're out in the fresh air. If you have the sudden urge to upchuck, you can aim for a bush."

"Ladies," the compere shouted, his voice hoarse with enthusiasm. "You don't have the luxury of refusing an invitation. You will have your turn to pick a gentleman tomorrow, and of course, you're welcome to spend time with any shifter during the other organized activities."

"Anita." Rory extended his hand. "You heard the man."

She muttered under her breath and stalked past him to join the others who'd chosen their partners.

Rory observed her angry strut as she preceded him. He wasn't stupid enough to smile. Instead, he handed her the list of the items they had to locate.

"We need a plan of attack," he said.

She scanned the list. "Outside items first, since we'll need to walk farther to find them. The inside items should be faster."

"I agree."

Soon they lined up and waited for the starter's gun. A loud boom echoed around them, and the couples surged forward.

"I passed an oak tree during my loch walk this morning," Anita said.

"Right. Are you up for a jog? We want to move as fast as we can without exhausting ourselves."

"Lead the way."

Rory thrilled at the competitive glint in her eyes, and he set a fast pace. It was a test of sorts since he wanted a strong woman. A sissy town girl would never pass his grandmother's high standards.

"What type of job do you do?" Rory asked.

"I'm a widow, and my husband left me fairly well off, but I work in a lawyer's office three days a week. I also help with community events in Middlemarch, where I live. What about you?"

"I make furniture."

"You do?" Her brows arched. "I don't know why, but I presumed you were a farmer."

"My family has always been farmers, but times are hard. Our people turned to woodwork during the cold winter months. We have talent, and it made me think about diversification. It has worked well, although there was resistance at first."

Rory noted she kept up with his pace, and pride filled him. She was robust and fit, yet feminine too. "Do you get the chance to run in your feline form where you live?"

"Yes." She didn't elaborate.

He tried again. "Is Middlemarch a good place to live?"

"It is. Our Feline Council works hard to give us everything we need yet keeps us safe. It was a fluke that led me to the town, but I'm glad I relied on my instinct to visit. It didn't take long for the town to feel like home, so I stayed."

Intrigued, Rory sought another topic to keep her talking. "If you find a mate here at the gathering, will you want to return to New Zealand?"

She shrugged and put on a burst of speed. "The oak tree is up ahead. Oh, look. A black feather. Isn't that on the list?"

Rory checked, and aye, it was. He plucked it off the path and placed it in the paper bag the organizers had handed each couple. "An acorn." He scooped one up and turned it over in his palm before placing it inside the bag. "What's next on the list?"

"A photo of a MacGregor headstone and a piece of pink heather."

Rory glanced around. "We'll have to walk up the hills behind the castle to collect a sprig of heather. Have you seen a cemetery?"

"No. Maybe we'll be able to spot it once we get higher."

She'd lost some of her reserve, and a healthy pink tinted her cheeks. It made Rory wonder what she'd look like during lovemaking. Heat roared through

54

him, and his wolf stirred, emitting a low growl. Rory restrained his wolf and raced to get ahead of Anita. A furtive approach might work best.

The second problem was he got the sense she didn't want to move to Scotland. So, he'd pick his battles and face them one at a time. He and his wolf were of an accord. They weren't about to let her escape with another shifter.

Chapter 7

No Change

"Where's your shadow?" Edwina asked in a whisper.

The Middlemarch six were sitting in Ye Olde Hawk, one of Glenkirk's pubs, each with a beer.

Anita glanced over her shoulder, an instinctive move she couldn't have stopped if she'd tried. Her stomach lurched, but thankfully, he wasn't there. The man discombobulated her, despite the years since she'd last seen him.

"He's not my shadow."

Anita turned to face her friends while fighting to maintain an impassive expression. Her breath whooshed out on seeing every one of them sported a broad grin.

Ramsay picked up his beer and leaned closer. "I don't know. Every time we turn around, he's there. I think he likes you."

"It's your imagination," Anita said, quashing her feline's inner purr of pleasure. Time to change the subject. "Has anyone met a potential match?"

"Not yet," Suzie said. "But it's only been one day. We shouldn't have sneaked off this afternoon. We owe it to Saber and London and the council to at least take part and represent Middlemarch."

"Let's make a pact to do that from tomorrow," Liam suggested. He was a newer resident of Middlemarch and worked on a local farm owned by a feline shifter family. "We agreed to give this a try because we like and respect Saber."

"Let's enjoy the evening, and tomorrow, we'll do everything expected and search for those fictional fated mates." Anita lifted her beer glass in a toast. "To tomorrow."

Each of them lifted their glasses and clicked them together. "Tomorrow."

"Your shadow has arrived." Ramsay spoke in an undertone after his gaze swept the crowded pub.

"You're teasing me." Anita snuck a glance over her shoulder and discovered Ramsay spoke the truth. She groaned. "I don't believe this." She tried to tell herself she wasn't pleased, but that was a lie. Each time she saw him, talked to him, hugged him, or rather he hugged her since they'd won second prize in the scavenger contest, it became more challenging to maintain her resentment.

It was difficult to recall why she disliked him and tough to blame him for the abrupt changes in her life and the break with her parents.

He drew her, attracted her, but stubbornly, she wanted this gathering to finish so she could return home with a clear conscience. She'd tell Saber she'd tried, but if fated mates were real and she had one, they hadn't been in attendance.

And that would be a lie.

Rory might've rejected her, but he was still her mate. She knew it, and it seemed as if Rory knew it too—given his behavior.

She drifted back to the past, the memories still sharp enough to hurt. Rory had stared at her while his grandmother's guards had closed ranks and pushed her back. Elizabeth Henderson had taken umbrage and burst forth with her outrage. The cheek of a scrawny feline. Anita was obviously after money since she didn't have two pennies to rub together. Rory would never lower himself to accept a nobody. *Her.*

Rory hadn't commented. He'd lifted his head, his nostrils had flared, and he'd turned away from her.

Anita recalled the scalding hot tears pouring down her cheeks. Silent tears that obscured her vision. Every one of Elizabeth's scathing barbs had cut deep, flaying Anita's confidence. She'd ordered Anita to leave and not show herself within the castle grounds ever again. At the time, Anita and her family had lived within the castle walls. She'd gone straight home and hidden in her bedroom, but her father had still lost his job that day.

The start of Anita's banishment.

Anita straightened, determined not to linger over past bitterness. This entire situation confused her because he'd rejected her, yet he didn't seem to think it was a big deal. He hadn't mentioned the bust-up. She absently took a sip of her beer and thought back. Actually, his behavior was weird. He was still acting as if he'd never seen her before.

Granted, she hadn't joined the dots for him, but he hadn't clicked on hearing her name.

Strange.

Perhaps the way he and his grandmother had treated her family embarrassed him, and he was uncertain of how to broach the matter.

Gah! Here he was, screwing with her thoughts and making her believe in the impossible all over again. Nothing had changed. *Nothing.*

They had no future.

Anita finished her beer.

"Want another one?" Ramsay asked.

"No, I'm heading back to the castle," Anita said. "I didn't sleep well last night. An early night might help to prepare me for tomorrow's activities. I need to psych myself into the right frame of mind to impress Saber."

"I'll walk back with you," Edwina said.

"Me too," Suzie said, standing. "We'll catch up with you guys tomorrow at breakfast. Will that work?"

"Fine by me," Liam said.

"Me too," Scott said, another new arrival in Middlemarch and one of Saber's cousins.

"It's a date," Ramsay said. "Want another beer?"

"My turn to buy the drinks," Liam said, bounding to his feet.

Anita sensed a stare but ignored Rory. A flash of anger replaced her confusion. This wasn't fair. He wasn't acting fair. She wasn't stupid enough to let him ruin her life a second time. No, she'd remain friendly and polite and nothing more. It was only a short visit.

Surely she could manage that without breaking her heart all over again.

Chapter 8

Musical Kisses

Rory had to force himself to let Anita leave the pub without his interference.

"Your grandmother expects you to mate with a wolf," Hugh, his head bodyguard, said, his voice mild but his expression stern.

"I'm aware." Rory clenched his fists to the point of pain and quelled the pithier retort trembling at his lips. "Beers all round? A pint of bitter?"

"We shouldnae be here," Hugh said. "It's not safe."

"The pub is full of shifters from the gathering," Rory said, keeping his tone mild.

The overprotection was unnecessary. His grandmother loved him, but he was no longer a child. He was an adult who'd steered the pack into the future. By any standards, they were wealthy now, and they were making a name with their furniture. He didn't need his grandmother to micromanage him. "I doubt anyone will attack me here. The confrontation happened years ago, and grandmother's elite guards caught the man who tried to kill me."

The idea of Anita at his side thrilled him. Her presence felt familiar and perfect.

It was as if he'd known her for years. Fleeting images dashed through his mind, but they were gone before he could decipher them. When he'd been in his early twenties, the strike on him had left him injured and bedridden for three months. Gradually, he'd recovered, but the head knock had left him with missing memory.

Their healer had informed him this was his body's way of coping with the shock, and his memories might never return. Not that this hampered him. His grandmother had told him he'd missed nothing of import—merely days of helping her with the sheep and cattle and the eating of a delicious joint of beef their cook had roasted. Everyone in the pack had mentioned the tasty meat.

"We'll have one beer and return to the castle. I want to speak to other shifters. It's interesting to hear how their species manage this modern world. It's not silly to listen to them because we require new markets for our furniture."

The bodyguard gave a reluctant nod, but his expression remained unhappy.

Rory gritted his teeth and struggled for patience, but it wasn't Hugh's fault. It was his grandmother's for butting in where she wasn't wanted and doing the overprotective thing. When he returned home, he needed to speak to her again and repeat that he would choose his life partner. Not her or anyone else.

Rory waited for his turn at the bar. When the barmaid turned to him, he said, "Four pints of bitter, please."

"Rory, isn't it?" a man asked. Anita's friend.

"Aye. You're Anita's friend."

"Ramsay. Don't hurt Anita. She has gone through enough, and she is happy now."

"I don't intend to hurt her," Rory snapped.

"See that you don't." Ramsay turned his back on Rory and smiled at a blonde woman standing beside him.

Rory sucked in a quick breath to calm his anger. Although it appeared Ramsay and Anita were close, he sensed nothing romantic between them. Anita had left while Ramsay had stayed and was talking with the blonde.

When Rory returned to the table where his body-guards sat, Hugh was on the phone.

"I'll do that," Hugh said, his gaze on Rory before he slipped his phone into his sporran.

Rory sighed. "How is Grandmother?"

"In her usual fine form," Hugh said.

"I see." Irritation flashed through Rory as he slid onto a wooden chair. This spying on him had to stop. However, there was no point in taking his anger out on Hugh when this was his grandmother's doing. He should've been firmer before he left. Hell, attending this gathering was a compromise. He'd backed down during their recent *discussion* instead of letting his temper rip. While he respected his grandmother and everything she'd done for him, it was time for her to butt out and let him live his life.

The pack was thriving, and several young men and a few women had taken up apprenticeships. Word of mouth had helped the business flourish, and with the advertising he'd arranged before he left his castle, this growth should continue.

"Is the bitter drinkable?" Rory managed an even tone.

"The beer is equal to the batches our brewer makes," his youngest guard said.

Rory's phone rang, and he snatched it off the tabletop to glance at the screen. His grandmother. He hit ignore and let the call go to voicemail.

"She'll keep calling until you speak to her," Hugh said, his gaze watchful.

"As much as I love my grandmother, she needs to trust me to do the best for our pack. No one goes hungry now. Our youngsters stay with the pack instead of leaving, and I believe we're successful. Am I wrong?"

"You're not wrong," Hugh said.

"Excellent. Report if you feel the need, but you will tell Grandmother I am participating in the activities and meeting wolf shifters. Don't give her specifics of the women I'm associating with or other personal details. Those are things I will tell her once I arrive home. If she tries to pull rank or threatens your positions on my staff, you will tell her nothing extra. I am the pack alpha, and your allegiance is to me. I'll remove you from my security team if you ignore these instructions. Do you understand?"

Rory met Hugh's impassive gaze and waited for an acknowledgment.

Hugh offered a clipped nod while the other two wolves stared at him.

"Do I have two heads?"

"Nay, alpha," one said while the other gave a vigorous nod.

"We will keep your activities confidential," the other said.

"Hugh?"

"Aye," Hugh said.

"Thank you." Rory picked up his beer and swallowed a generous mouthful. It was excellent and a fitting way to celebrate him laying down the law. His grandmother would fight him, but she wouldn't win.

When he finished his beer, he stood. "That's me for the night."

The three men rose.

"You have my permission to have another beer. It's a ten-minute walk, and I have my phone should I encounter problems."

The men dithered, and Rory bit back a grin.

"Look," Rory said, "when I was a child, a security team to keep me safe made sense, especially after Grandmother received the death threats. Since I've taken over, I haven't faced problems. I highly doubt anyone followed us here. It'd be difficult to sneak around with this many shifters. Also, the security is tight at the gathering. No one gains access without an official invitation. Please, stay. What Grandmother dinna ken won't hurt her."

After this speech, Rory exited the pub without glancing back.

To his relief, none of his team trotted after him. He scanned the vicinity and caught the scents of the pub patrons—the bite of sweat, cheap aftershave, and a teasing note of Anita's flowers.

The woman acted like a skittish deer, but he savored a challenge. Tomorrow, he'd learn which activities she planned to attend and make sure he put himself in front of her. Now that he'd decided to pursue her, the last thing he wanted was competition.

The woman belonged to him, even if she fought him now.

Rory strode the short distance to the castle and found an activity underway. He grinned because it looked as if Anita was playing, and it wasn't too late for him to join this game.

Rory drifted to the rear of a line of male shifters.

An announcement crackled through the loudspeaker—the compere again, decked out in an eye-grabbing sparkly tartan. "Ladies, you will remain in your seats and leave them arranged precisely how we have them. This is important. This game is a little like musical chairs with kissing.

"When the music starts, the gentlemen will stride toward you in a line. When the music halts, a gentleman will pause in front of each of you. They will smile and do nothing else if they are not interested in pursuing a relationship with you. If they might be interested but aren't certain yet, they will kiss your cheek and move on to the next lady. If you think this lady is your fated mate, please kiss her on the lips and hold her as if you're never letting her go."

Faint laughter greeted this.

Rory studied the women. There were around twenty-five participants. The compere blasted a horn, and the first man strutted forward to the music. His position at the rear might be problematic, but he'd go with that. At least he might get to kiss Anita. He waved as he passed the first woman and blew her a kiss.

The bystanders laughed and cheered, and the man sauntered onward.

Gradually, the waiting men joined the parade, and the audience cheered. The ladies flirted, fluttering their lashes and puckering their lips. The male shifters lapped it up, creating much laughter with their shenanigans. Soon, it was Rory's turn, and he strode toward the first shifter female—a wolf. He winked at her when the music continued. The music stopped when Rory was halfway along the line of chairs. He hadn't reached Anita yet and didn't think she realized he was partaking in the game.

"Gentlemen, turn to face the beautiful lady in front of you. Remember, you can smile, kiss her cheek, or lay one on her. It's up to you and your shifter half to determine if she could be the one for you."

Rory smiled at the woman, who faced him with a trace of anxiety. He'd hate to embarrass her, but he didn't want to encourage hope when there was none. Anita was the one for him.

He smiled at the bear shifter, a large, curvy woman. She wasn't attractive—more striking, with her bright blue eyes and long curly black hair. He blew her a kiss, and she winked at him in return.

A roar lifted the roof, and Rory spotted a man laying a hot and heavy kiss on a petite blonde. She wasn't arguing, but was kissing him right back.

The onlookers cheered.

"We have an early winner," the compere spoke over the suggestive comments that flew quick and salty through the room. "Our first couple so far? Am I right?"

Rory didn't care. He wanted to continue the walk and let fate decide if he could kiss Anita tonight.

"Congratulations," the compere shouted again. "Please see my efficient and delectable hostess here, and she will give you a special prize."

Rory's curiosity rose since most couples in his pack were not fated mates. They rubbed along well enough, but he'd heard proper mates had something special binding them together, making their relationship magical. Since he had little experience with the mate concept, he remained a little skeptical.

The couple walked near Rory on their way to speak with the hostess. His quick sniff told him they were wolves. The woman took shaky breaths while the male blinked rapidly, yet it was easy to discern their happiness. Their glow. The male had his arm wrapped around his mate's waist, and a distinct growl rumbled up his throat when another shifter male stumbled too close.

Huh! *Interesting*. Maybe he shouldn't dismiss the mate concept so fast because Anita did draw him.

The compere tested his mic with a rapid tap-tap of his fingers. "Ready to go again?"

A male shifter in front of Rory pumped his fist into the air. "Yes."

His enthusiasm had Rory grinning.

The music recommenced, and Rory's heart raced as he rounded the end of the first line of women and started back. Each step took him closer to Anita. Her two friends sat on either side of her, and they were flirting big time. Anita looked as if she was frowning, but she still hadn't spotted him.

The music ceased. Rory came face-to-face with one of Anita's friends. He couldn't recall her name, but she snuck a glance at Anita before grinning at him and puckering up.

Rory laughed aloud, dipped his head in acknowledgment, and grinned back.

The music started straightaway, and Rory glanced at Anita. He saw she was staring back in distinct apprehension. The music halted, and the compere cackled at the instant confusion because every male had only advanced one spot.

Rory turned toward Anita, who was staring at him in horror. His inner wolf growled. Oh hell. Was she crying?

An urgent need to comfort her and ease her distress propelled him close enough to place his hands on her shoulders. A shudder ran through her, and he witnessed her audible swallow. His wolf growled again, but soft enough for only him to hear. Every part of Rory craved her kiss and to stake his claim. He leaned nearer, tuning out the laughter, the chatter, the surrounding hilarity. He dragged in a breath full of her flowery perfume and the faint muskiness of her feline.

Their feline.

He struggled to control his wolf, to wonder at the terror in her expression. What filled her with trepidation when the two of them were so right? Every fathom of his being, every thought, reiterated they were mates, that he was wrong with his doubts. And crazily, there was something familiar about her, yet

71

he couldn't put this sense of *knowing* into context. He stared into her brown eyes, his wolf compelling him to show her he was her mate and master. He was her alpha.

Their gazes connected. Clung. But one overriding thing became apparent to Rory.

Anita didn't want him in the same way he craved her.

He froze, hesitating, and at the last moment, he jerked to the left and placed his lips against her silky cheek. Her shoulders slumped as he stepped back. His wolf growled, the sound full of anger, but Anita's gaze held thanks. Relief.

The music burst into life again, and his feet propelled him forward.

All he could think was that Anita Gatto was his fated mate, and she didn't want him.

She'd rejected them—him and his wolf, and that was a crime.

Chapter 9

Not My Mate

Relief struck Anita like hard, icy rain at Rory's hesitation. She implored him with her eyes, trying to tell him without words they could never be together. He'd rejected her once, and he'd do it again in a heartbeat if his grandmother had her way. Rory might be the alpha wolf, but his grandmother held an extraordinary power of her own, and from the little Rory had told her to date, she assumed he took advice from Elizabeth.

Elizabeth Henderson would take one look at Anita and see beyond her carefully constructed mask. She'd discern the nobody feline girl—the one Rory had rejected and helped to cast from pack lands without regret.

Anita sensed the internal warring in Rory. Glimpsed his wolf, flicking in his eyes. Until the very last moment, he'd intended to kiss her square on the mouth. He'd planned to claim her, and no! No, that couldn't happen.

He'd diverted his lips and kissed her on the cheek. Her heart leaped against her breastbone, her feline as edgy as her. She no longer paid attention to the music, her entire being focusing on Rory's where-abouts. What was he doing? Why was he chasing her now when he'd rejected her in front of his pack?

The surprise element made her uneasy. Her hands trembled. Her legs, too, and she was glad she was sitting rather than standing.

The situation made no sense.

The game continued, and she received smiles but no more kisses.

"Well, that was a bust," Edwina said once the game ended, and the competitors dispersed to the bar or the dining room for a late supper.

"That guy you vomited on," Suzie said, her mouth pursed as if she were deep in thought. "I watched his expression when the music stopped. He was going to kiss you, then changed his mind. I could see the magnetic pull between you. Rory is your mate."

"No!" Anita groaned because her instant denial fanned the flames of suspicion in her friends. They might be younger than her, but that didn't make them stupid.

Edwina claimed Anita's hand and towed her over to a private alcove, occupied by an old set of armor. "Right. Spill."

"Don't worry. The armor won't tell tales, and neither will we." Suzie offered her an impish grin.

Anita groaned again. "Long story short, I knew Rory when I was a teen. He's ignoring that fact, or he doesn't remember. I don't know which is worse."

Edwina's neatly plucked brows drew together. "Why is that such a problem? It's obvious he's attracted to you, and you're not immune. The two of you light up when you're together. My bet is you're mates."

"No!" Anita snapped. "His grandmother disapproves of me, and it's way better if I return to Middlemarch and forget about Rory. I'm hungry and craving something sweet. Anyone else want to check out the desserts?" A lie. She was in danger of choking if she tried to eat anything, given the apprehension lodged in her throat.

All she could think of was Rory and how much she ached for his touch. His kiss. His c— Anita cut that thought dead and barely restrained a sensual shudder. She lifted her head and strode to the bar without waiting for her friends. She'd have a drink at the very least—perhaps something containing alcohol to help her sleep.

The next morning, after a sleepless night, Anita crawled out of bed and took a cold shower. The slap of frigid water didn't shock away her drowsiness. She'd only seen her roommate on the first night and presumed she'd found other accommodations. Not that the lack of company bothered Anita.

She chose casual black slacks and a short-sleeved red and white blouse since the outfit always made her feel vibrant and in control. A façade and one she was perfecting this week.

The truth—her mind refused to trot past Rory. She'd dreamed of him last night. A nice slice of happy slumber until the dream had morphed into a replay of the day she'd declared Rory her mate.

She recalled the horror on everyone's face at the top table. The disgust and the fury displayed by Rory's grandmother. The ridicule and jeering laughter that had come from the wealthy men and women, their daughters. Why would he show favoritism toward a scrawny, ugly feline shifter when he could have any one of the stunning, curvy werewolf daughters?

Even worse, Rory had remained silent and done nothing to defend her—a rejection in itself.

Yeah, she'd awoken with a scream and her heart pounding while tears poured over her cheeks. Today, she'd stay far from Rory. All she needed to do was get through the next few days.

When she could no longer dawdle, Anita sighed and left her room. The other Middlemarch shifters had secured a table, and she joined them, thankful she could be herself during breakfast at least.

"Coffee," Anita croaked once she'd taken her seat.

Scott grinned at her. "Tough night?"

"Bad dreams," Anita said, keeping it simple. "Where's Ramsay?"

"He wasn't there when I got out of bed. Either he had an early start, or he didn't come home."

"He was still at the pub when we left," Edwina said.

Suzie took a long sip of her tea. "Should we worry?"

Anita considered, pausing while she topped up her coffee. "He's an adult. I'll text him if we don't see him by lunchtime."

"Maybe he met someone," Edwina said. "You know I'm kind of envious when I see the couples. Saber told us we wouldn't necessarily find our one, but a part of me craves the whole deal."

To Anita's surprise, Suzie nodded in agreement. When Anita tested her feelings about Edwina's confession, she realized she wanted the same. Difficult when her fated mate had rejected her and was

77

now playing confusing games. As far as she knew, a shifter didn't have more than one fated mate, but who knew? Mating seemed a complicated business.

She chugged her coffee, praying the caffeine boost would jolt her awake. "What's on today? I forgot to look."

"A couple of mixer events and more contests, so we get to know other shifters," Edwina said.

Before Anita could reply, the compere appeared at the door with the purple microphone that seemed an extension of his flamboyant personality.

"Good morning, ladies and gentlemen. I hope you slept well because we have a busy schedule today. But before I remind you of the details, I want to let you know we have six shifter couples who've discovered each other. Six! That's a record for this early in the gathering. Let's give our couples a round of applause!"

Anita clapped with polite restraint, but several shifters around the dining room whooped and cheered, rising and stomping their feet in celebration.

When everyone settled, the compere said, "We're hoping for more mates today, and with that in mind, those shifters who played musical kisses last night—if you kissed a woman on the cheek or a man kissed you on the cheek, we've arranged a special picnic for you. The waitresses have your picnic basket and taped to the top, you'll find details of your private spot where you can get to know each other better."

Anita issued a groan, and it was loud enough to make Suzie and Edwina grin.

"Snared," Suzie whispered.

Edwina glanced across the room and back to Anita. "Rory is grinning and looking in this direction. He likes the idea of getting you alone."

"Oh shut up," Anita muttered, refusing to check on Rory's reaction to the news.

"All those shifters who received kisses or kissed cheeks stand up. Don't be shy. I have your names. Don't make me read them out to get you hustling."

With another mutter, Anita gulped the last of her coffee and stood. Across the room, Rory did the same, but she would not look at him. *She would not*. Anita shot him a side-eye before she could stop herself. He wasn't smiling or smug. Instead, his posture was strong, movements precise, and he radiated determination.

"Good morning, Anita," Rory said when he reached her. "I'll collect our basket and destination." He strode to the two perky hostesses and waited in line. One consulted her list and smiled at Rory. Anita couldn't see his expression, but jealousy punched through her, hard enough to leave her breathless and in shock.

No, this wouldn't do.

She had to control her feline before she did something stupid.

Rory returned and glanced at her strappy sandals. "Change your shoes. We have a bit of a hike before we reach our waterfall."

"We could just not go," Anita said.

"I considered that, but if we take a selfie of both of us in front of the waterfall, we'll go into a drawing to win a tropical holiday," Rory said. "We might as well enjoy a walk through the forest, get some fresh pine-scented air, have a delicious lunch in excellent company, and use the time to learn more about each other."

"Don't we know enough now?" Anita asked with an impatient shrug.

"We talked the other night, but I want to learn more," Rory said easily. "I'll meet you out the front in ten minutes. I'm going to grab another coffee."

Anita stared after him. What the hell? She'd grown up around the pack. Sure, her appearance was different, but her scent would remain the same. Wolves were excellent trackers. Her claim on him had been very public. How could that horrendous day fade from his memory when the events burned

into hers like a permanent tattoo of the worst moment of her life?

Chapter 10

A Private Picnic

Rory carried the picnic basket and led the way along a track. They came to a signpost pointing toward the waterfall, and Rory shoved the directions into his pocket.

Anita's sure steps followed him, and he was ultra-aware of her presence. Her floral perfume floated to him—essence of Anita. Today, when they relaxed after eating lunch, he intended to kiss her and show her he was more than interested.

The thought had immediate repercussions for his body. Every part of him tensed at the idea of touching her. During their kiss, he'd let his hands wander unless she offered an objection or shoved him away. He didn't think she'd protest, given her furtive glances when she thought he wasn't aware.

"What do you do for fun at home?" he asked.

"Swim in the river. Ski during the winter. I enjoy baking and cake decorating. Reading. The feline community has regular runs in the backcountry." She glanced back at him, and something about the way she cocked her head struck him as familiar.

He stilled halfway through a step and tripped over a stone when he focused on her. Aye, something about her teased him, but when he tried to follow his thought, all he could see was a blankness that did nothing to answer his questions. Frowning, he continued after her. He'd noticed her accent came and went, and sometimes it held a hint of Scottish.

"Are you certain you haven't been to Scotland before?"

"Yes."

A definitive yes, but why had she lied? Somehow, he knew with total certainty this wasn't her first time in Scotland, despite her words to the contrary. Rory pondered this and let it go for now.

"Tell me more about this furniture of yours. Do you have plans to expand, or do you get enough work and orders from your local town?"

He saw what she was doing—deflecting by changing the subject. Two could play at this game. "I'm happy for you to learn more about me, but I should get to know you, too. How about taking turns with the questions?"

"I thought that was what we were doing?"

A smooth reply with nary a pause, yet she didn't fool Rory. Still, once again, he let her sidestep and pondered her familiarity. His guards hadn't recognized her. Not that he'd asked them, but they would've mentioned it. Besides, no feline families lived near Castle Henderson.

"We have expansion plans and have started an advertising campaign to bring in more orders. Our strength lies in the solid artistry and the fact each piece is unique and designed for the recipient. This means we can charge a top price for our product. Word of mouth is big for us, and our craft is in demand from homeowners who want to renovate their 17th and 18th-century buildings. We received an order to construct a carved wooden banister for a staircase before I left."

"Who's keeping the business running while you're at the gathering?"

"My best friend, Marcus, is a carpenter, and we set up the business together. He is more than capable of keeping everything running while I am away."

"Marcus," she said, and he looked askance on hearing her strange tone.

"Have you met Marcus?"

"No."

Her reply, instead of reassuring him, raised his hackles. Something reeked of two-day-old fish in this scenario, and Rory couldn't figure out what it was or why she was prevaricating. Perhaps he should ask one of his team to investigate her. He considered this for all of two seconds and discarded the idea. No, not now. If she wasn't more forthcoming soon, he might go that route. But he'd feel happier if the information he sought came from her.

Sneaky and underhand—that was his grandmother's style, and he'd spoken to her more than once about this, telling her this way was not his. He preferred an open and honest approach.

"How long should this walk take?" Anita broke into his thoughts.

"The instructions showed around two and a half hours. I guess they want to make sure each couple has total privacy."

Anita mumbled something under her breath that Rory didn't catch, but he grinned at her stiff back, unaccountably enjoying her burst of temper.

"Aren't you enjoying the walk?" he asked. "I would've thought if you work in an office, you'd relish this chance to get outside in the fresh air."

"I told you, I get lots of opportunities to run in my cat form. Our local Feline Council is active, and they make sure we can safely exercise our cats. Also, where we live is sparsely populated, so we don't face city dweller problems."

Interesting. When they spoke about general things, Anita became quite chatty. Only when he directed the conversation into personal did she clam up and give him one-word untruths.

"Are you spending long in Scotland, or are you returning home straight after the gathering?"

"Saber booked us a week in Edinburgh so we can sightsee and experience city life as well as here at Glenkirk. The six of us in our group get on well together. It should be a blast in Edinburgh, doing touristy things and shopping for friends and family at home. What about you?"

"I'm heading straight home since we had several big orders come in. Marcus says he can cope, but it will be easier for everyone if I'm there."

A loud crash on the path in front had them stilling and throwing out their senses. Anita lifted her head and dragged the air deep into her lungs. He did the same.

"Deer," Anita said.

"Aye, we must've given it a fright."

They continued walking along the marked path, the dead pine needles muting the thud of their boots. The fresh scent of pine filled the air, and

Rory caught the gurgle of a mountain stream, but it was somewhere out of sight.

"Do you want to stop for a drink?" he asked.

"Sure."

Rory set down the picnic basket and pulled one of the attached water bottles off the side. He opened it and handed it to Anita. Surreptitiously, he watched her and the way her throat worked as she swallowed. His gaze settled on the fleshy spot at the base of her neck where wolves marked their mates. God, he wanted to do that to her in the worst possible way. And that was only the first on his long list of things he'd love to do with Anita Gatto.

He must've made a sound because she paused and lowered the bottle. "Aren't you having a drink?"

"I thought we'd share," he said while trying to will his body to obedience. His wolf, now, that was another matter. A low growl escaped Rory without his volition.

Anita scowled. "There's no need to get testy about it. All you needed to do was ask or tell me what you intended."

She thrust the water bottle at his chest, and Rory took it with nerveless fingers. *Get a grip, man. This one is skittish, and if you want to win her, you need to woo her. Throttle back.*

"Thanks," he said, aiming for casual. He drank down the water without tasting it and finished the bottle. "Did you want more?"

"I can wait until we get to the waterfall."

Water wasn't the only thing they'd wait for until reaching the waterfall. Every time he glimpsed that pouty pink mouth, he wanted to savor. He craved...he wanted touching rights—the freedom to run his fingertips over that smooth skin, to test the silkiness of her hair. That was all he'd allowed himself to think at this stage, but it was damn hard not to let his gaze wander her shapely form. Walking behind her and watching her round arse move beneath the pair of jeans she wore was turning his dick to stone.

In desperation, he diverted his thoughts to work and the pack. His grandmother.

Yeah, that did the trick.

The rush of water grew louder, which told Rory they'd almost reached the waterfall. Anticipation built in him as they rounded a corner. Water tumbled over rocks, dropping around eight feet to the round pool below. The outlet ran over more rocks, fell into a valley, and disappeared. Trees surrounded the pool, but a small grassy clearing made the area perfect for a picnic. Somewhere in the distance, an owl hooted, and closer, smaller birds tweeted and flitted from branch to branch.

"It's a lovely spot," Anita said, her body language contradicting her words. She held her muscles tense as if she wanted to flee rather than relax.

"Are you frightened of me?"

She froze, her gaze fixing on him. "No."

"Then why are you behaving as if I'm about to attack you? And you realize that running isn't a good idea, anyway?" Rory forced a grin. "My wolf would impel me to chase."

"Haha," Anita muttered.

"Do you not trust yourself with me? Are you tempted to jump me and have your wicked way?" Rory opened the picnic basket and drew out a red-and-black tartan square. He spread it out on the ground and gestured for her to sit. She sat as far from him as possible, making it necessary for her to stretch to her full extent to accept the bottle of water he handed her. His mouth twisted. "You don't seem to trust yourself."

Anita snorted. "I can resist you."

"Prove it," he snapped back.

"How?" She took a sip of water, her throat working as she swallowed.

"Kiss me." Rory let the dare simmer in the air between them. "Kiss me and prove you can resist my Highland charms."

Chapter 11

Cat Got Ya Tongue

"Highland charm, my arse," Anita muttered before she could think better of her outburst.

"You're frightened of the possibilities between us, which is why you keep pushing me away. Who hurt you in the past? Your husband?"

Anita spluttered. The arrogant, no-good wolf. How could he sit there and pretend he didn't recall his rejection? Was it any wonder she wanted to leap from her skin? It was a constant war with her feline because now that they'd reencountered Rory, all she wanted was to jump him and seduce the too handsome, too arrogant, too sexy Scotsman.

"Cat got ya tongue?"

Anita's temper flared, and she pounced before her brain slotted into gear. Rory fell back with an *oomph*, and she landed on top of him. Seconds later, she ground her mouth against his until she caught a hint of blood. It was the coppery flavor on her tongue that shoved sense back, and she retreated.

Rory pressed a finger to his mouth and dabbed at the blood. "Wow, if that's how you operate, it's no wonder you're still single."

"Oh, you...you..."

"I'll show you how it's done," he said, his eyes gleaming.

An instant later, she was flat on her back with Rory looming over her. He stared down at her, and the humor in his features just pissed her off. She attempted to wriggle free, but he lowered his head and caressed her lips with his. It was a slight contact, but a powerful one and every scrap of fight seeped from her. Once she relaxed beneath him, he deepened the kiss, taking it into sensual territory. Mouths caressed and tasted. Tongues touched and explored, and throughout it all, one truth battered her over the head.

He was her destined mate, but how could they have a future when he'd rejected her?

The anxiety returned and faded, chased away by the stroke of his callused finger, delicately stroking her cheek. His touch sizzled clear to her toes, frisking over parts in between and leaving her craving more of his decadent contact. The man had skills, and she groaned, twisting beneath him until their bodies aligned perfectly.

Rory rubbed his nose against hers. She inhaled the scent of the soap he'd used in the shower and his underlying wolf. It was like catnip—a dangerous drug she couldn't escape, not now that they'd kissed.

"I suspected our coming together would be spectacular," he whispered, seconds before he kissed her again. Their legs tangled, and Rory took greater liberties.

Huh! Not that she tried to stop him. She'd turned into putty in his experienced hands, more turned on than she'd ever been with her husband.

He cupped her face with his big, work-rough palms and teased her lips before he began his seductive plundering. He devoured her mouth while his hands wandered lower.

Before she knew it, the buttons on her cotton blouse were open, baring the swells of her breasts to his gaze. His appreciative gaze. The wolf wasn't shy about showing her his desire, and the easy way he played her body and turned her molten with lust didn't go unnoted. His prior experience. A flash of jealousy darted her before Rory offered distraction with the nibble of teeth. He mouthed the mating site, that fleshy pad at the base of her shoulder. A tingle spread from that point and consumed her. She groaned, the first genuine sound she'd made.

He lifted his head immediately. "Ah, I'd wondered if I'd receive a verbal reaction."

"Don't be a dick."

"Have I proved we have a bond between us and our shifter halves want each other? Or do I need to go further?"

Yes, please. She stared at him, lost in his beautiful eyes, before Rory's soft chuckle jerked her back. "No, point proven. I'm hungry. Could we eat?"

He studied her for a beat longer before pushing away from her heated, sensitized body. An immediate protest formed on her lips, and she struggled to silence her feline and the urge to grip his shoulders and haul him back against her. The lack of contact had her fingers twitching and a shudder tap-dancing down her spine. *No! It wasn't meant to happen like this.*

"I'm returning to New Zealand after the gathering." Her words were those of a sulky child with something to prove.

"I understand." His voice was even, and she failed to read him.

Enigmatic Rory.

He opened the basket again to peruse the contents. "Ah, we have smoked salmon sandwiches, according to the label. And a bottle of wine. Would you like a glass?" He peered at the label. "New Zealand sauvignon blanc. A taste of home for you."

"Is it a Marlborough wine?"

"You're in luck." Rory busied himself opening the wine while Anita unwrapped the parcel of sandwiches and selected one. The saltiness of the salmon contrasted with a citrus tang as she bit into the granary bread. Delicious.

Aware of the pulsing silence, Anita swallowed the last bite and cast her mind for something to say. "Why do you want to kiss me?" Not quite the topic she wanted. It'd lead to more awkward questions.

He glanced at her, a furrow between his brows. "Why wouldn't I? That's the better question. You're smart and sexy and not a kid. You have life experience, you're gorgeous, and my wolf wants you. I'm in step with my beast on this. I desire you, too. Are those enough reasons?"

A lump grew in her throat as resentment filled her. His rejection had changed her entire life course. How could he pretend nothing had happened?

"You rejected me," she snapped, unable to hold her tongue for an instant longer. "I approached and informed you we were mates, but you spurned me." Fury pumped through her as the memories swamped her.

He froze, his toothy smile stuck in place. His eyes bulged, and a wolfish growl scratched up his throat, emerging in clear agitation. She glowered when he continued to eye her as if she'd arrived from another planet.

"What? No comment?" Anita leaped to her feet and prowled across the clearing to ease the restless angst punching her mind, her body, her feline. She shot him a glare, shocked yet not surprised either by his non-reaction. He possessed a lot of his managing grandmother in him, or at least that was the way it appeared to her. Well, she refused to let anyone direct her ever again. She'd had that with Rory's grandmother, her parents, and then her husband. Anita enjoyed her freedom and giving it up for an arsehole who'd suddenly decided they were mates was nowhere on her agenda.

"What are you talking about," Rory demanded.

When she shot him a scowl, she spotted his knitted brows, his frown.

Rory rose and crossed the grass to reach her. "When did I reject you?"

"You didn't even have the guts to face me, to speak to me. Instead, your grandmother hustled me from the castle, and a week later, we were moving south and my dad taking a job in England. Two weeks after that, I was a married woman and on my way to New Zealand." The hot words spilled from her while she observed him through narrowed eyes.

He clasped her hand, and her traitorous heart flip-flopped. Her pulse quickened when his fingers tightened on hers. She tried to wrench free, but he held her fast.

"Please explain. When did this happen? My grandmother has never mentioned it."

Anita's eyes rounded. "You were there. Don't tell me you weren't because I spoke to you. It was dinner, and everyone was in the Grand Hall. When I told you of our mate status, you stared at me as if I were something nasty on the bottom of your shoe. Your grandmother took over and kicked me out. My parents lost their jobs."

"Who were your parents?"

Anita gaped, momentarily speechless. At first, she thought he was kidding because how could he not recall the confrontation? But he didn't laugh. He didn't sneer or say the joke was on her. He genuinely didn't remember the pivotal moment that had changed her entire life.

"Your parents?" he prodded.

"Ross and Blair Lennox. My father worked on the estate as a gillie, and my mother worked in the castle as the housekeeper."

"Lennox. I remember them," Rory said slowly, his brow furrowing. "They left to take up a new job."

"Your grandmother forced us from the castle." Anita wrenched her hand from his and stormed over to pick up her daypack. She compressed her lips and kept her nasty responses internalized when he remained silent. She shrugged into her pack and turned to him. "I'm returning to the gathering." With that, she stomped from the clearing and strode along the path that led back to the castle.

A woman could only take so much rejection.

Chapter 12

Rory Faces The Past

Every instinct urged Rory to follow Anita, but confusion held him back. He remembered Ross and Blair Lennox, and he distinctly recalled his grandmother telling him another employer had poached them by offering more money and improved conditions. A *Sassenach*.

But Anita...

He cast his mind back, but not a single memory of her sprang to mind.

She'd accused him of rejecting her.

They were mates—of that, he had little doubt, which meant somehow, he had to fix this mess. If he'd truly rejected her, why couldn't he remember? Had this happened before the attack?

Rory repacked the picnic basket but decided to run in his wolf form. He rarely had a chance for a solitary run since his security team trailed him everywhere.

His grandmother held secrets, but he'd prefer not to speak with her yet. He required information. His security team might have the knowledge he sought or the older members of his grandmother's security team.

He shucked his clothes, and just as his shift took him, his phone rang. *Nay.* He'd return calls after his run. Perhaps by then, he'd have a better plan for wooing Anita. Rory called up his wolf and let the shift slide over him. Bones cracked and muscles reshaped. Reddish-brown fur poured over human skin. His senses exploded, everything about his surroundings becoming more intense.

Rory padded off the path, the leaf litter and pine needles cool beneath his paws. He lifted his nose to the breeze, caught a rabbit's scent, and loped deeper into the forest.

His run filled him with newfound confidence and determination, and when he arrived back at the waterfall, he took a quick dip in the pool. Cold but refreshing water pebbled his skin and washed away dirt and sweat. Dressed again, Rory picked up the basket and strode toward the castle.

His first task would be to locate his security team and question them. Depending on their answers, he'd make a plan to woo Anita to his way of thinking. Only after that would he confront his grandmother.

Hugh found him, falling into step as Rory headed to the kitchen to hand off the picnic basket.

"How was your day?" Hugh asked, searching Rory's expression before glancing away.

"Didn't go the way I expected."

"You came back alone," Hugh said.

"I want to talk, but not here. We'll speak in my room where there is no danger of eavesdroppers."

Hugh shot him a scowl. "Did you call your grandmother?"

"No."

"She wishes to speak with you."

"Is there a problem with the pack?" Rory asked.

"Nay."

"Then there is no reason for me to have a discussion with my grandmother," Rory said, struggling to keep his voice even. He opened the door to his bedroom and gestured Hugh inside.

Hugh frowned. "Are you attending the mixer this evening?"

"Aye." Since he was here at the gathering, it would make sense to meet more women. He couldn't explain his attraction to Anita and refused to discuss it with anyone apart from her. The truth—he wanted her. He wanted to spend time with her, but he'd be an idiot if he ignored this opportunity to converse or dance with other shifters. At the very least, it'd help him understand his attraction to the feline.

Contacting others would prove his wolf wasn't leading him astray, and Anita Gatto was his mate. This was his human side talking, but they were a team. Aye, confirming this in his mind would be a smart move.

Rory's phone rang again, and he ignored it, setting it on the nightstand.

"Hugh, what do you know about Ross and Blair Lennox?"

Hugh blinked and scowled at Rory's phone, which started ringing yet again. "Who?"

"Hugh, you're older than me and have worked for the security team for years. Don't play dumb." Anita hadn't lied to him about her parents because the wounds had been obvious and still raw. No one lied that well.

Hugh cleared his throat. "I gave your grandmother an oath."

Rory inhaled and sought calm. Of course, his grandmother stood amid this fiasco. "Anita Gatto nee Lennox says she is my mate, that I publicly rejected her. I have questions. Why the hell do I not remember this? I don't recall the moment, nor do I know what Ross and Blair and their daughter Anita looked like. It's funny, but Anita drew me from the moment we met, and she vomited over my favorite kilt. Sometimes I thought she was familiar, but I couldn't grasp the memories."

"I didna recognize her at first," Hugh said.

Now we're getting somewhere. "So what Anita told me is true?"

"I canna talk to you about this."

Rory straightened. "Right. You tell my grandmother this. Anita is my mate, and I will do my best to sway her to my way of thinking. And if Grandmother argues, please inform her I am the alpha wolf, and what I say goes."

Hugh's face paled, and his mouth worked several times before speaking. "It might be best if you spoke to your grandmother and asked your questions. Please don't make me break my oath. A man's honor is important, aye?"

"What about my honor?" Rory asked. "Years ago, I rejected Anita. I don't recall the circumstances, and now she's gun-shy because of my past behavior."

"Ask yer grandmother."

"If you won't tell me anything further, I have no use for you. Hugh, you and the security team, can return home. I don't need you here spying on me."

Heat crawled into Hugh's cheeks. "Is that an order?"

"It is," Rory said. "Things will change once I return home. I refuse to put up with my grandmother micromanaging me. I was the one who single-handedly clawed the pack back from the point of ruin. It is my furniture-making hobby that helps the pack thrive now. I care for those in our pack, but I realize the pack's allegiance isn't to me."

"We show you loyalty," Hugh snapped.

"Not true. You show my grandmother loyalty. You answer to her and sneak around behind my back. It's she who makes the decisions, and because I'm busy organizing our business and working, I let her have her way. I see now I've blundered in allowing this. Now, get out of my sight. Go home."

"But what if you need us?"

"If I get into trouble, one of the hundreds of shifters at the gathering is bound to show charity and offer aid."

Hugh's shoulders slumped, and he left the room. If he'd been in his wolf form, his ears would've drooped, and his tail would've tucked between his rear legs. Rory had never pulled rank in this way. He was easygoing and did his best for the pack, protecting the weak and keeping the strong in check. Everyone had plenty of food, and Rory ensured they were financially secure. He'd hired teachers to educate the young wolves and gave each shifter in his pack a chance to develop their strengths and gather knowledge. He'd improved conditions and took pride in that fact, yet it appeared his hard work had gone unnoticed and unappreciated.

No more.

Rory left his room, not bothering to pocket his phone. He'd find a group of shifters to keep him company. He didn't care what they were as long as they were friendly, which was how he ended up drinking shots in the late afternoon with seven bear shifters and some of the male contingent from Middlemarch. Anita's friend Ramsay wasn't there, but Rory liked the other two felines. Scott and Liam were farmers and new to Middlemarch, but they enjoyed the friendly locals and took part in the many functions and activities their feline leaders organized for them.

The bears came from Canada in the main, but one or two Russians filled out the group.

"Anyone found a mate yet or someone they'd considering spending more time with?" a Canadian bear asked.

Rory shook his head, but his wolf growled low and menacingly inside his mind. His fingers curved to claws, and tension slid across his body.

"I'm convinced these gatherings do nothing. I mean, what is their success rate? My alpha insisted I attend, convinced I'd find the one," a Russian bear said.

"The alpha wanted a week of peace," one of his friends shot back.

Rory didn't add to the conversation, his mind slipping to Anita. Hugh's reaction told him Anita hadn't lied. She and her family had lived with his pack for several years, and then they hadn't. He sighed, facing the indisputable truth. It was time to face down his grandmother, and he needed to do it in person. This internal power struggle had to cease. His pack didn't respect him. Hugh's behavior had proved this. Rory was alpha, yet Hugh remained loyal to Rory's grandmother.

This had to stop. It was time for a change, but his first obstacle was Anita. He rose abruptly and left in search of the lovely shifter. Time to meet her wrath.

Chapter 13

Arrogant, Pompous Dog

Not even stomping down the mountain path at speed calmed Anita. Her nostrils flared as audible breaths heaved up from her chest and out of her mouth. Sweat coated her skin, and she was practically grinding her teeth by the time she flung open her bedroom door and clomped inside.

The arrogant, pompous dog!

She'd told him the truth, and he'd looked at her as if she was a talking head that had popped out of nowhere.

"Dirty fleabag." She flung off her clothes and stalked to the en suite.

During her shower, she pondered the ways she could damage him. A fist to his pretty face. A punch in the gut. Or better, a swift kick to the balls. Her feline prickled beneath her skin as agitated as Anita with the uppity mutt who thought himself so far above them he'd rejected her. And worst of all—now he was pretending he didn't remember the callous act.

She turned off the water and grabbed a towel to blot the water off her skin. That done, she pulled on one of the complimentary robes and strode out to the bedroom to collect her phone. *Ramsay*.

She'd call her friend. Maybe he could talk her down because she wanted to pack her bags and head for the airport right now. And that would disappoint Saber. Saber Mitchell was a feline she liked and respected, and the last thing she wanted was to renege on her promise to him and the Feline Council.

Ramsay's phone went to voicemail.

She hung up with a frown. What was up with him? She hadn't seen him since last night, and that was strange.

A knock at the door had her springing to her feet. She jerked the door open before using her senses to test the air and almost crashed into Rory.

"I don't want to talk to you." Anita attempted to slam the door in his face.

"Please, I won't bother you for long. I want information."

When Anita took a second to study him more closely, she noted his pale features, the way he fidgeted. But he met her gaze, and it was this openness and glimpse of his confusion that had her tamping down her anger and jumbled hurt. She inhaled and released the breath slowly while giving herself time to think.

"What sort of information?" Suspicion laced her tone, and she counseled herself to act with caution. She didn't intend to make this easy for him.

"Can we talk inside your room? Please?"

Wordlessly, she stepped back, and Rory entered her room, the fragrance of soap and a freshly showered man floating in the air. His kilt swished with each purposeful step. The space shrunk with him in it, although he did nothing to ramp up her unease.

"Sit over there." She pointed at her roommate's bed, the one unused for the last two nights.

Rory backed up and gave her space. "First, I want to apologize. I know you're telling the truth, but I don't remember any of the events." He swallowed hard. "I haven't spoken to my grandmother yet, but I did question Hugh, who is head of my security team."

"And?" Anita prompted, eager to hear what he'd say and learn how he'd twist the truth when he'd rejected her and turned her into an outcast in her home country.

"He refused to tell me what happened and told me to speak to my grandmother."

"Your grandmother is a formidable lady. She made it clear no grandson or clansman of hers would sully themselves with a non-wolf shifter." Anita snapped out the words, still feeling the sting of hostility all these years later. When Elizabeth Henderson had ripped Anita away from Rory, she'd broken something. Anita had tried to enjoy her new life and forgive those who'd separated her from her mate. She'd survived—barely—and didn't think she was strong enough to repeat the ordeal.

Rory jerked upright and glared at her. "I am not my grandmother."

They stared at one another, and hope and yearning broke in Anita, even though she tried to control the compulsion to comfort him. An instant later, Rory stood so close they were almost touching.

"I want you. All of you. I don't understand any of this, and we'll get to the truth, but know this. When I saw you in the Great Hall, you snared my interest. Every part of you fascinates me, and the layers I've uncovered so far tell me you're an amazing woman.

Any shifter male would be proud to have you stand at their side. You're strong and compassionate. You care about your friends and community. I hope you have a corner in your heart for me because I intend to prove I'm worthy of the spot."

A lump formed in Anita's throat, and hope surged before she tamped it down. Words. They were just words. Empty promises that didn't mean a thing. It was actions that mattered most.

"Please give me a chance to prove I'm not all hot air."

Anita shook her head. "We have no future. You live in the Highlands. It's your home. You're the alpha of your pack, and they need you and your strength and foresight to survive. Your grandmother made it clear I'm not welcome, and the truth is I don't want to return. The Highlands are no longer my home. I've fallen in love with Middlemarch and its residents. They're friends and support me. If I ever have problems, I have help, and I offer aid in the same way. It's a genuine community with a common purpose to stay safe in this modern world and to live rather than merely survive."

"I love the Highlands."

"That's my point. We have no future."

"Anita." Rory purred her name. His big, callused hands cupped her face. He stared deep into her eyes, and she saw his wolf reflected at her. He touched his lips to hers, and she stiffened until he employed gentleness and coaxing. His fingers skimmed her back and settled on her hips. Rory deepened the kiss, and Anita found herself powerless to stop him. Her feline purred with satisfaction, ecstatic to have the mutt kissing her now when she'd been spitting and agitated earlier.

Anita tried to step away and opened her mouth to speak and object. Nothing happened. Instead, she sighed and locked her hands around his neck, pressing their bodies closer until his chest crushed her breasts.

The kiss morphed from sweet to demanding, sweeping Anita along with the firestorm. She forgot her objections, hurt feelings, and anger and let herself wallow in the desire and the sensation of powerful arms surrounding her. Protecting her.

Anita closed her eyes and felt herself floating because Rory had swept her into his arms and placed her on the bed. His hands skimmed with purpose, with skill while he continued his assault on her mouth. Right where she wanted to be, she decided, and the loud purr from her feline confirmed this thought. Even if they couldn't be together, they could have this one snatched moment.

Something for her to recall on those quiet nights when she was alone. Or at least that's what she told herself.

"Anita," he said, breaking their kiss. "You're sweet. So addictive." He pushed out a heavy breath and pressed his forehead to hers. "We should talk more before we go further. Can you tell me what happened back then?"

Anita stared up at him, taking in his blue eyes and his brown hair with its hints of red. She ignored his request, not wanting to end the magic that bubbled through her. She reached up to run her fingers over his stubbled jaw. "No talking. Not now. Rory, no amount of talking can fix this. We want different things. Can't we enjoy this moment together?" She was almost surprised to hear her words, then went for it. She'd have sex with him, and tomorrow, she'd walk away knowing she'd done the right thing.

For her.

For both of them.

A furrow appeared between his brows, and she thought he might argue. He stared at her for a fraction longer before shaking his head. "This is probably a huge mistake, but I'm desperate to touch you, to make love to you." And saying nothing more, he lowered his head. His breath caressed her cheek, then their lips collided, clung. A hungry little noise escaped Anita, but she was beyond caring.

All she wanted was him.

Consequences be dammed.

The sleek thrust of his tongue against hers told her he was getting with the program. The sultry promise in the stroke of his hands and his hot intent gained her approval. Her feline's too.

"Too many clothes," she gasped.

Rory's eyes glowed, his wolf close to the surface. He levered away from her and unbuttoned his shirt. After shrugging it off, he unfastened his kilt and tossed it aside. He wore nothing beneath his tartan, and Anita admired the work-hard muscles as he returned to the bed. His erect cock displayed his desire for her.

"Your turn to undress. I'll help." His hand hovered over the belt of the robe she wore, his eyes seeking permission.

"Yes."

The belt loosened, aided by a tug. Then his hands smoothed the toweling fabric aside to reveal her breasts and torso.

"Lift for me," he whispered, and soon, she was as naked as him.

His gaze ran over her, leaving a tingling, prickling trail on her skin. He drew a breath, the ragged sound snaring her attention, and his hand trembled as he reached out to touch her.

"So beautiful," he said. "I'm not sure where to start."

"Everywhere," Anita whispered. "Touch me everywhere."

He swirled his fingers down her rib cage, and her heart lurched painfully. Rory eased himself back onto the bed and took a moment to kiss her again. She fell into the contact, and it took a second before she realized he'd cupped one breast while he invaded her mouth. His earthy, masculine scent surrounded her, leaving her aching for so much more. Sultry passion filled his features while he explored her breasts. Soon warm heat covered one globe, and he tongued her nipple, teasing it to a hard point.

Anita ran her hand down his back, testing his muscles, her fingers coming to rest on his butt. She squeezed and couldn't help but grin with satisfaction.

Rory laughed and sucked on her nipple. Hard. Her breaths grew shallow, her stomach hollowed, and a moan rolled up her throat. She clenched her thighs together and fought the begging words that tried to escape. She wanted him—yes—but...

"Stop thinking. Let me show you how good we can be together. Please."

Their gazes connected, the atmosphere electric between them.

"I can stop. We can get dressed and go our separate ways. Never see each other again."

"No." The word emerged before her brain engaged. She opened her mouth again to tell him she'd changed her mind. He should go. *No.* No, that wasn't what she wanted. "Please don't go. We should at least..."

"Follow the passion between us."

"Yes," Anita whispered.

"Are you always this indecisive?"

"No."

He grinned and kissed one pouting nipple before the humor left his face, and seriousness took over. Primal hunger flashed in his eyes, and Anita's pulse jumped into a racy beat. He levered over her and parted her legs with a muscular thigh.

"I can smell your arousal, lass." His Scottish accent was broader and more compelling now.

"Yes." Because what more could she say? She lusted for him. Yeah, this was all about desire and carnal pleasure. *Sure, tell yourself that, Anita.* She forced her mind onto a different path because these doubt demons were passion killers.

Rory moved down the bed and cupped her buttocks, lifting her to his mouth. The first lick sent her flying, the slight roughness of his tongue coiling a sensual ache in her belly. He sucked at her clit, giving her gentle pressure as if he understood what she liked without her telling him. He slid one thick finger inside her and set up a rhythm. Everything in her grew tight and continued contracting until it became too much. The strum over her clit combined with the internal caress of his fingers, had her flying. Her orgasm broke, engulfing her in flaming pleasure. It took her long moments to float down and for her wits to return.

"Wow." She offered Rory a tentative smile. "That was something."

"Hold on, lass. We're only at the start of our journey."

Chapter 14

Sweet Loving

The taste of her flooded his mouth, and she was a sight to behold. Her long black hair fanned across the pillow while her golden-brown eyes held a trace of shock and bewilderment. But there was pleasure too—a look he wanted to see again soon.

"Are there condoms in the nightstand drawer?"

She frowned, and he regretted the need to introduce the mundane contraception topic. With the turmoil between them, an unplanned pregnancy would be disastrous. A child's arrival should fill parents with joy and excitement. Not hostility and secrets.

"I guess. Not sure," Anita added. "It isn't an issue for me since our local feline doctor gave us girls shots designed to halt pregnancy."

"No condom?"

"It's unnecessary."

"Thank you." Rory kissed her lips gently before he fitted his cock to her entrance. He took a quick breath because this was a momentous step. He couldn't explain his hope and excitement—it was more a gut sensation. His wolf-half was equally transfixed and plain thrilled to spend time with Anita. Making love and skin to skin was even better.

Rory snatched another kiss even as he pushed into her. Scorching heat and tightness greeted him, gripping his cock and stealing his breath. He rocked his pelvis forward and glided into her until he was balls deep. Anita groaned, and mentally, he duplicated the sound, the pure rightness of this act hitting him on every primal level.

"Are you okay?"

"Move," Anita ordered.

"Aye, lass." Rory withdrew and powered back into her.

Her internal muscles flexed and rippled around his length. Impossible to take his time, but maybe if she enjoyed this, she'd want to repeat the experience. Rory set a frenetic pace, and she gripped his shoulders and held on tight. Her hips lifted into his strokes while an emotional storm flared around them.

"Can you come like this?" he asked, desperately trying to slow his body's race to climax. His balls drew up, and his cock swelled.

"Not normally."

Rory had the sudden urge to bite her, to mark her, and join them in the traditional way. The idea clandestinely slid into his brain, but his wolf intercepted the notion and ran with it. Rory kissed Anita and nibbled down her neck to where his kind marked their mates. He bit down before he realized what he was doing. Horrified, he forced himself to release her and kissed the upper curve of one breast instead. Anita moaned and shuddered beneath him. He pinched her breast hard, and she cried out. At first, he thought he'd hurt her.

"Again," she ordered. "Roll my nipple. Give me a hint of pain."

He followed her instructions, and her internal muscles clamped down on his dick. Rory couldn't hold on for an instant longer.

"Come for me, please. I can't wait." He pushed into her, and it was too late. He was way past the point of no return. Balls deep, he poured his release into her. She released a sharp cry, and his cock jerked when she tightened around him. The tiny pulses prolonged his orgasm, and satisfaction slashed through him.

Content and replete, he held her while trying to keep his weight off her. Without warning, his cock jerked, and it felt as if it were lengthening even further and burrowing into Anita's flesh. Some sort of protrusion. A barb?

Rory cursed under his breath when Anita flinched. He tried to pull out of her, but their bodies remained connected.

"Fuck," he muttered.

"What is it? What's wrong?" Anita's brown eyes were wide, and her cat hovered close to the surface.

"We seem to be attached." Rory thought back, trying to dig all the tales from the depths of his mind. He'd thought it was nothing more than imagination and gossip. "Have you heard any rumors about matings that take place at the gathering?"

"No."

"The history of the gathering comes with a warning. According to the room brochure, there is speculation that those mates who make love in the castle have an extra something. It's said they knot together to ensure a fruitful mating."

Rory watched Anita's expression the entire time he spoke. She turned from relaxed and satisfied to startled and tense.

"That can't be true." She wriggled her hips, and a distinct tug ran through Rory's cock. "Crap. At least

I can't get pregnant. How long do you think this enforced togetherness will last?"

"I didn't believe what I read. Urban legend, and all that. It sounded like a made-up story for romantics. A sales pitch by the organizers."

"What does this mean?" The stiff edge to Anita's voice and her tense muscles told Rory she wasn't happy while elation filled him. Best if he didn't show that exhilaration at present.

"It's nature's way of confirming we're true mates, even though I'm a wolf and you're a leopard."

"I'm not staying in Scotland. After the gathering, I'm going to Edinburgh with my friends and returning to Middlemarch."

Just the thought of parting from her pushed anxiety into Rory, although he concealed his emotions and plastered on a poker face. He chose the expression he used while addressing pack youngsters about their pranks when he wanted to cackle aloud at their ingenuity. It was the one he also employed with his grandmother when she was attempting to tell him what to do—for the pack's good.

Sudden fear nipped at Rory. What if Anita didn't want to make love with him again? Now that he'd had her, tasted her, he craved more. It was time to consolidate their relationship foundations for the future.

"I sent my security detail home," he said, the words flying from his mouth.

The irritation fled from her face, and she grew attentive. Okay. Maybe he'd tell her what he was thinking and go from there. He'd had no one to discuss pack business with apart from his grandmother, and she continued to tug at the reins even though he was officially in charge. He'd made a mistake at the beginning, not stamping his authority on the pack.

"Why did you do that?"

"I learned Hugh, the head of my security, is reporting to my grandmother. It's not as if I need a security team. Times have changed. To fit in with modern society, we can't have wars between species. Not if we wish to blend. I doubt if anyone would take over my pack for our wealth. We have the land, but most of it is mountainous and unproductive. We farm and we hunt, but that wasn't enough to survive. I told you earlier—that's why I specialized in furniture building and taught our pack youngsters a trade."

"Your grandmother has always wielded power. I was aware of that from the moment I declared myself to you. She hustled me away from you so fast I suffered from whiplash."

"I need to confront my grandmother. It hasn't mattered that she hovers and second-guesses my decisions. This is my fault. It didn't bother me as long as I could keep doing the things I enjoyed. All I wanted was to make my furniture and ensure my pack thrived."

Rory sensed an easing of the barb and gave his hips an experimental wriggle. He felt the weight of a stare and met Anita's brown gaze.

"Kiss me?"

"Aye." That was a simple decision for Rory. Their lips slid together, and warmth suffused him. The rightness of having her in his arms. His erection eased, and he withdrew a fraction, discovering freedom of movement. Rory retreated before filling her again.

Anita rocked into his thrust, sighing as if the gentle move offered great pleasure. Arousal burst through Rory again, his dick filling and growing hard enough for a repeat performance. Since Anita didn't seem to object, he set up an effortless surge and retreat, teasing them both until the heavy fog of desire swept them into a place where sensation ruled. This time, his release was more gentle but no less fulfilling. Anita didn't come before him or with him, so he withdrew and licked her until she climaxed with a hearty groan.

"We didn't lock together this time."

"No. I'll try to learn more about this, hopefully without receiving nosy questions in return," Rory said.

"Do you want to share a shower?"

"You're not kicking me out?"

"No. Not yet." Her mouth twisted as she rolled to her feet. "For some reason, I find myself reluctant to part from you. My feline," she added.

Rory nodded, not wanting to upset the fragile peace between them, but he made a silent promise that he'd speak with his grandmother soon. He tossed up calling her, then decided his original plan was best. He needed to see her in person and use every one of his wolf's senses to determine if she was lying to him.

Chapter 15

Rumblings Of The Past

What the heck was she doing? This wolf couldn't be part of her future. They were worlds apart. *Literally.*

Rory reached past her to flip on the shower. It was funny, but the first time she'd used this shower, she'd imagined it was big enough for two. Now Anita had proof there was ample room for both of them. She stepped under the water, pulling the door closed after her. The steamy heat struck her skin, easing well-used muscles. She tilted back her head and let the water wash over her face. Rory edged behind her until his warmth cradled her back. He reached for the soap and a loofah, and once he'd created a lather, he swirled it over her breasts and stomach.

She let him.

She shouldn't, but it was such a luxury to have someone care for her.

"Move forward a fraction so I can do your back."

Anita stepped out of the water flow and presented her back to him. The trouble was, she could imagine a future with him. This togetherness was so simple, yet she knew better.

Nothing was ever easy.

"Hey, stop thinking so hard." He dragged the loofah down her spine before crowding her against the wall. The loofah splatted to the floor, and his fingers stroked her folds. He strummed her clit, and excitement roared to life. After that, she stopped thinking because Rory pinned her and fucked her until nothing but the raw energy of lust and sex remained.

With shaking legs and a raft of goosebumps on her arms and legs from the now cool water, she left the shower stall. Before she could pick up a towel, Rory was there, enfolding her with warmness and taking care of her.

"It's almost time for dinner," he said.

"The formal is tonight. I don't feel like getting glammed up and socializing. I haven't been sleeping well."

"Then we won't go," Rory replied. "I'll call the kitchen and ask if I can collect two meals to eat in our room. We don't have to take part. We're adults."

Anita sighed. They were mature, which meant they had to make the hard decisions. After tonight, they'd need to part because even the idea of a future with Rory was too problematic. Elizabeth Henderson would never accept Anita. *Never.* She'd made that clear in her cutting remarks on that ill-fated day so long ago.

"You're nothing. A nobody," Elizabeth had spat at Anita.

Anita had been crying hysterically, her feline on edge and her control on low. Her claws had pushed past the tips of her fingernails, and sharp canines had made speech difficult.

"You're a worker and can never be part of my pack. You are a common baggage with ideas above your station and more attitude than good sense. Rory is a leader, destined for great things, and with the right woman at his side, he'll be unstoppable. Leave the pack lands, or I will have you executed."

Even now, Anita's heart beat faster on remembering those stark words. Elizabeth had not been kidding. Anita had threatened her plans—a scheme that had not come to fruition despite Elizabeth's maneuvering.

"Why haven't you ever united with another wolf?"

"I've never met one I wanted to keep." Truth rang in his instant reply. "That's one reason." Rory ran the towel over his torso before propelling Anita into the bedroom.

"There's another reason?" Anita peeked over her shoulder and discovered Rory ogling her butt. She rolled her eyes at him.

"The pack wasn't doing well when I took over from my father. They needed my focus, so I worked hard on survival strategies. Most evenings, I was too tired to entertain a woman since I planned to lead from the front."

Anita frowned. "What happened to your father? Your mother? When I left the pack with my family, they were still around."

"My father was never strong mentally, and my grandmother put him under a great deal of pressure. She prefers things done in a certain way and treats pack members like chess pieces."

Anita made a noncommittal sound, and Rory's lips twisted.

"My grandmother is dominant and expects everyone to follow orders. Those who don't move fast enough end up steamrollered. Collateral damage. Even though he was her son, my father wasn't resilient enough, which is why she focused on me. Unfortunately, instead of telling her to pull in her head, I've let her continue unchecked. I've countermanded her orders behind the scenes to keep the peace. In hindsight, that was a mistake because she's still interfering in my life."

"You still didn't say what happened to your parents."

"They moved to Italy, where my father manages an orchard and grows grapes for a hobby. They're much happier away from the pack. My mother has taken up painting. I visit them once or twice a year."

Anita pulled on the robe that she picked up off the floor.

"Do we need to dress?" Rory asked.

Anita ignored this to ask more questions. "What happened? Why did your parents leave?"

"My grandmother." Rory ran a hand through his hair, leaving the damp strands sticking up in tufts. "She organized a bride for me. This was years ago. It can't have been long after you left because I was barely twenty. The she-wolf came from a European pack, and I disliked her on sight. Her scent was wrong, and she was a carbon copy of my grandmother in attitude and behavior." He shook himself. "I haven't thought about this for years. The memories are blurry." He paused again, appearing to consider something, and his brow furrowed. "I can't remember much, but I refused to go ahead. My parents stood up for me, and my grandmother was furious. She was offering a way forward for the pack, a way to increase our finances and survive, and couldn't understand why I didn't jump on her plan. She and my father went off for a walk, and when they returned, my father told me he was giving me control of the pack. I could make my decisions and do what I wanted, what my grandmother wanted because he was done. He couldn't continue living this way. I didn't speak with either of my parents for two years." He rubbed his hand over his face. "The entire situation has a dreamlike feel to it, and my memory of events in the prior weeks is blank. Evidently, I was sick after the attack, and it took me a long time to recover."

Anita's stomach gave a loud rumble. "Pardon me." She rose and pulled her handbag out from under the bed. After several minutes of rifling through it, she pulled out a sad-looking chocolate bar. "Want some?"

Rory laughed and donned his kilt. "I'll order from the kitchen. Want a bottle of wine as well?"

"Sure."

"You drink white, right? A sav blanc?"

"You pay attention."

Rory drew nearer and cupped her face with his hands. An instant later, he was kissing her with tenderness. He lifted his head and stared into her eyes. "Of course, I pay attention. You're a beautiful woman, and I wanted to get to know you better. I'll grab clean clothes from my room before I organize our meals. Won't be long."

Rory let himself out the door, and it clicked shut behind him, leaving Anita time to think over everything he'd told her or inferred about his life in the Highlands.

His hazy memories seemed strange, and his confusion when it came to her was apparent. She believed he didn't remember her and wasn't playing games. But she didn't understand. He'd known her. Not well, but enough to say hello or share a smile.

The first time she'd seen him, she'd been fourteen. Small and scrawny, but a feisty fighter. She'd rescued a wild kitten from a group of older boys tormenting it. Rory had come along to stop them from beating her. That had been when she'd fallen for him. She'd been shy with boys, but with Rory, she'd stammered her thanks and taken the kitten home.

It'd been hero-worship. She understood that from the distance of time.

But after that meeting, she'd watched for Rory. She'd observed him running in his wolf form and flirting with the she-wolves. She'd spotted him toiling alongside the pack carpenter. He'd worked hard, and when she'd spied on him, he'd been undertaking pack duties. Obviously, his grandmother and father had groomed him to take over. Had Rory known? From what he'd said, his parents' defection to Italy had come as a surprise.

Anita ate the chocolate bar and straightened the bed. On impulse, she called Ramsay, but his phone clicked to voicemail. She shrugged and left a message, telling him she was spending time with Rory. Her friend would be happy for her.

A quick tap came on her door, but before she reached it, Rory entered. He carried a bottle of wine and two glasses.

"The cook told me she'd get two meals delivered."

"Aren't they busy with the formal night?"

Rory shook his head. "They have extra staff." The rattle of a trolley had him poking his head back out the door. "Here it comes now."

"That was quick," Anita said.

"What can I say? I used my charm."

Anita smiled, but it didn't feel natural. Rory possessed great charisma, and Anita feared she wasn't immune to it. Already, they'd made love twice and that knotting thing. That was beyond crazy and so hard to wrap her head around. No, she had nothing to fear. Just a few more days of friendship and enjoyment and hot lovin', then they'd part forever.

Chapter 16

A Promising Future

Anita grew quiet during their dinner, but Rory suspected fatigue was the culprit. Lethargy was a problem for him. He hadn't slept well since arriving at the gathering and spotting Anita. The woman filled his dreams, sleeping and waking, and now welcomed him into her bed, into her body.

His mate.

Even though he still needed to face his grandmother and wrestle back control, joy suffused him. This showdown had hovered on the horizon for some time, but he'd known any disagreement between them would cause ripples throughout the pack.

"Not hungry?" he asked.

"I was, but now I'm tired." She shoved aside her plate.

Rory removed the partially eaten plate of roast beef before turning back to Anita. "Can I tempt you to have a few bites of dessert?"

Anita perked up, and he hid his amusement. "Chocolate?"

"The kitchen staff gave us two portions of Death by Chocolate cake plus clotted cream on the side."

Her grin was a thing of beauty, which he accepted as approval. Rory picked up one portion of the cake, along with a spoon. "Let's share and save the other for a midnight snack."

"Are you staying the night?"

"Aye, if that works for you." Rory met her gaze, only relaxing once he spotted her acquiescence. Thank God. He wanted to spend every moment with her and learn the small things that made her unique.

"It's fine. Dessert." Her eyes sparkled with enthusiasm.

He dug into the cake and offered her the first bite. She closed her pink lips around the spoon. Her eyes fluttered closed, and she made a humming sound.

Every muscle in Rory pulled tight, and he barely restrained his lustful groan. "How is it?" he asked, his voice hoarse.

Her eyes popped open. "Delicious."

Without taking his gaze off her, he took a mouthful of dessert for himself. Chocolate and cocoa, featherlight mousse, and crunchy shards exploded across his taste buds.

"Am I right?" Her voice was low and husky and pushed his mind to long nights of satisfying sex.

"Aye, lass."

They devoured the dessert mouthful by mouthful, never taking their gazes off each other. When they'd scraped the plate clean, they were breathing hard, and arousal swirled in the air. *The best foreplay ever.*

Rory stood and extended his hand. She placed her fingers in his, and he led her to the bed. He kissed her, slow and unhurried while exploring her mouth. Their breaths emerged in gasps by the time their lips parted. Rory worked her robe tie free and slipped the toweling off her shoulders. The fabric pooled at their feet.

"Let me help you undress," she whispered.

Their hands collided, the process not exactly graceful, but soon they were naked. Rory scooped her off her feet and set her on the mattress, following her down. Their lips met, and their arms came around each other. Their lovemaking was slow and sweet, a symphony of strokes and intimate touches that soothed Rory's wolf even as it aroused him. He nuzzled her neck beneath the curtain of black hair and lashed his tongue over the silky flesh. Despite the temptation, he avoided the marking site because Anita's uncertainty was clear.

He could hardly blame her if what she'd told him was true. Rory experienced difficulty imagining the cruel rejection, but with his grandmother, anything was possible. His lack of memories of the event bothered him, but he boxed his worry and shoved it to the edges of his mind. Time for investigations later. Instead, he'd focus on Anita's acceptance of him and bestowing the mating mark to connect them irrevocably as mates.

This feeling, the yearning, the rightness of their mating, was too important to make a fumble.

He took her mouth again and savored her happy sigh, the way she relaxed against him, her body soft and pliable. This time, he dawdled, exploring her rib cage, her tummy button, and testing the smooth skin of her inner thighs. Her unique flavor exploded over him. Her scent of flowers and feline and a faint hint of him. He inhaled that scent, wanting to recall it later when he was alone.

"Rory."

Her faint complaint made him smile. "Shush, lass. We'll get there soon."

To appease her, he shifted position and lifted her to his mouth. He teased her clit but didn't give her too much stimulation.

"I'm strong," she warned. "I could grab you by the ears and make you pleasure me. My strength is equal to yours."

His wolf growled while Rory grinned. "And if my wolf and I decide you should eat your words?"

"My cat and I say you should try. We're not delicate freakin' flowers."

"I see. A standoff." His laughter puffed warm air over her clit, and a noticeable shiver ran through her. A whine escaped his wolf, a reminder for him to hurry because they were depriving themselves, as well as Anita. This time, he licked with more purpose, and she rewarded him with a surge of moisture. He lapped and sucked at her clit until Anita shuddered under his ministrations.

"Yes," she muttered, squirming beneath him.

Rory smiled against her flesh and slipped two fingers inside her. She groaned and raised her hips, silently urging him to do more. Aye, it was time. He upped his pace, curling his fingers to find the particular spot to drive her crazy. His tongue ran over her swollen nub, the hard dig of her fingernails into his back telling him she was ready. This time, he massaged with fingers and sucked simultaneously. Anita flew apart, unraveling as he tended to her needs. He eased back when her flesh ceased spasming and licked her honey off his fingers. *Delicious.*

"Rory," she said. "Again. I ache and need you again."

Surprised but pleased, he moved up the bed to kiss her. He guided his cock into position and slipped into her scalding heat. Rory stroked balls deep and pulled back, the driving thrusts sending his need spiraling.

"Yes, perfect," Anita said, grasping his shoulders.

The play of emotions over her face pleased him—she wanted him as much as he craved her.

Rory drove into her, increasing his speed, seeking completion. He no longer had control, and his hips jerked with the hard strokes. Anita kept up with him, rising to meet each hard digging thrust. A thick slice of pleasure shunted from his balls and along his shaft, and an instant later, he exploded. His cock expanded and dug into Anita's flesh, attaching and connecting them again.

Anita's channel squeezed his shaft, the firm grip stealing his thoughts. Instead, all he could do was feel. A groan escaped him, his cock pulsing, the over-the-top sensations continuing for long moments. He was aware of Anita crying out, convulsing around his length.

Neither speaking nor moving, they held each other while their bodies remained connected. Anita must've dozed off because when his experimental tug let him, he could withdraw, and she never moved.

He didn't understand the magic between them, but he refused to give up or walk away. Rory intended to fight for Anita, fight for their future, even if it meant walking away from his pack.

Chapter 17

Gathering Activities

Anita woke refreshed and alert and lying in Rory's arms. A dozen emotions slapped her over the face. Astonishment. Happiness. Panic was the predominant one, but there were others too. Fear slithered into prominence. Was this a dream? Anxiety stepped up next because Rory's grandmother terrified her, and she'd hate a repeat experience of her teenage trauma.

She lay there, listening to Rory's even breaths, loath to move because she felt so comfortable.

"I'm awake," Rory murmured, his lips curving in a sweet smile. "What time is it?"

"Breakfast time." Her stomach backed this up with a loud grumble.

"I could eat," Rory said. "Why don't I shower in my room, and I'll meet you back here in half an hour? Is that long enough for you?"

Anita snorted. "I have my morning routine down pat. I trained with children, shuttling them to school and other activities. My skills are unsurpassed."

"I'm afraid I'll have to test you." Rory pulled on his discarded clothes.

"Thirty minutes," Anita said. "Don't be late."

Anita powered into action as soon as the door clicked shut, and Rory's quick knock came as she was applying her coral-colored lipstick. She picked up her handbag and opened the door.

"What's on today?" Rory asked when they fell into step, their bodies touching casually, which appeased Anita's feline.

"They usually slide the program under the door, but I didn't see one. We can check while we're having breakfast. The compere usually comes in and does his spiel each morning."

"Not many people around."

Anita glanced up and down the corridor and didn't spot a soul. "Maybe we've missed something important."

Rory shrugged. "Too bad. I'm where I want to be. Nothing else matters."

His casual yet telling words resonated with her. Now that they'd made love and spent time together, positivity filled her. When doubts surfaced in quiet moments, she tried to send them winging on their way. Rory's grandmother... She shoved the niggle away and focused on the now.

When they approached the dining room, a meaty bacon and sausage aroma filled the air, along with that of freshly baked bread. The hum of voices, the clatter of plates, and the clink of silverware indicated others were eating breakfast.

"I can't remember feeling so hungry," Anita said.

Rory reached for her hand and squeezed it. He kept his hold as they walked into the dining room. He led her straight to the buffet line and handed her a plate before taking one for himself.

Anita turned to waves and wide grins from Suzie and Edwina. They pointed at the empty seats at their table in an invitation to sit with them.

"Do you mind if we sit with my friends?" she asked.

Rory grinned. "I'd like that."

She searched his face. "You mean it."

"I do. I have questions about Middlemarch. Let's see if you exaggerated or if their answers tally with yours. You might be telling me fibs." His lips quivered with restrained merriment, so she didn't take umbrage.

"Middlemarch is a country town. It's close to the city of Dunedin, but it's isolated too. We have wilderness and mountains. It's very different from your Highlands but equally beautiful. For me, it's the people who make Middlemarch. The residents work together, and we have a solid community." Anita placed three rashers of bacon, a black pudding, and a sausage on her plate.

"Scrambled eggs?" Rory asked.

"Please."

With laden plates, they headed to the table where Edwina and Suzie were already halfway through their breakfasts.

"You're later than usual," Suzie said with an arch grin. Her green eyes twinkled while her dark eyebrows waggled like a comedian's.

"We slept late," Rory said without cracking a smile.

"I see." Edwina popped a piece of sausage into her mouth and chewed.

"Stop teasing us," Anita said, sliding into the seat Rory had pulled out for her. "Thank you."

"What's up today?" Rory asked. "Where is everyone?"

"Last night, they organized an impromptu run in the mountains. Most shifters took advantage to transform and tear around the great outdoors. We stayed here for the peace," Suzie said.

"Enough about that." Edwina pushed her empty plate away and topped up her tea. "I want to know about you two. The last time I saw you together, Anita was bristling like a porcupine. What's changed?"

Rory glanced at her, and when she didn't leap into the conversation, he answered the question. "We're mates."

"Anita?" Suzie asked.

"Yes, that's true," she said, focusing on her meal.

"Obvious to anyone with eyes," Suzie said. "What does this mean for your future? What happens next?"

Rory placed his hand on Anita's knee. "We're taking this one day at a time. We have history, and we're trying to work past the issues this has caused." He met Anita's gaze. "We haven't had a chance to discuss this yet, but that's what I want. A future with Anita."

"But what—" Edwina broke off abruptly with a yelp. She glared at Suzie.

Anita grinned. "Thank you, Suzie. What are today's activities?"

"This morning is a lazy one since the group stayed outdoors all night, and they were organizing a breakfast for them. Edwina and I were talking about the treasure hunt. We need a team of four, so join us. We have to find clues, and they're all outside. The prize is another tropical island holiday. If we win, Edwina and I might donate the vacation to you."

"What do you say?" Rory asked. "How do you feel about a holiday in the sun? Drinks. Swimming. Lazy nights. Good food."

"Enough!" Edwina clapped her hands over her ears. "I can't take hearing about your sex life when I don't have one."

"What she said." Suzie nodded emphatically.

"So we're a well-oiled team, intent on a mission to get Anita and me a holiday?"

Edwina and Suzie shared a glance. "We are," they chorused.

Even though most attendees had gone on the overnight run, there were still fifty or sixty shifters waiting to receive instructions at the starting point.

The compere arrived, resplendent in a red-and-blue tartan suit. Two scantily clad women trotted after him.

Beside her, Rory released a snort.

"Not your style," Edwina murmured.

"Give me a kilt anytime," Rory said.

Suzie winked, her gaze dropping to his feet. "You make a fine figure."

"Enough perving at Rory's legs." Anita didn't think she'd ever experienced this bubbling happiness before. A small voice warned her this wouldn't be easy. They had obstacles ahead. Right now, the trouble seemed less significant, so she'd try not to worry about it. She'd simply enjoy spending time with Rory and stress about the future once the gathering ended.

"I bet you're eager to get started," the compere shouted and cupped his hand to his ear. "What? I can't hear you!"

"Yes!" everyone shouted.

"Right. My lovely assistants have the first clue to distribute to every team. Once you solve the puzzle in the first clue, you'll find the next one. There are ten clues, which will have you exploring the castle grounds, the loch shoreline, and the forest beyond. You won't find any clues hidden inside the castle. I'll tell you that now. The deadline for the hunt is midday, when we will have a delicious barbecue lunch, followed by the prize-giving. I'm sure I won't need to give you any clues to discover our lunch location since you're all shifters. If you fail this, please hand in your shifter card as you leave."

Laughter followed this comment.

"Please form your teams of four and select one person to collect the clue from our lovely assistants. Keep it orderly, please. No pushing and shoving. We have enough clues for everyone, and no one can begin the hunt until I fire the starter's gun."

"I'll line up for the clue," Rory said. "You ladies work out our strategy."

He was gone only a few minutes. Anita, Edwina, and Suzie crowded around him to read over his shoulder. "What do you think? Any ideas of where to start?"

"Make a wish, but don't take a drink," Suzie murmured. "That sounds like something with water."

"One last rule," the compere shouted. "You must hold hands to start and finish the hunt the same way. Any team who finishes with all the answers to their clues must cross the finish line with their four players holding hands. After all, this week is about togetherness and making friends. I will disqualify any team that does not follow this rule."

"Where does the hunt end?" someone shouted.

"Follow your noses toward the barbecue, and you'll find the completion line. The first team over the line in the prescribed manner will win the tropical island holiday plus a bottle of bubbles to help celebrate their win. Any more questions? No? All right then. On your marks."

"When can we release hands?" a woman asked.

"As soon as you can no longer see me. If you can see my wondrous tartan suit, then you'd better be holding hands."

"Great," Rory mumbled.

Anita grinned because most of the comments were far ruder.

"Quick. Hold hands," Edwina instructed. "We'll start and think on the trot."

"You make a wish in a fountain," Rory said as they awkwardly stumbled along in a connected line while trying to avoid the other competitors.

Rory's touch warmed her heart, and optimism flowed in Anita. "Anyone remember seeing a fountain?"

Edwina wrinkled her nose. "No."

"The obvious place is the garden." Suzie turned their line in that way.

"Great, head around the back so we can drop hands," Edwina said. "I feel ridiculous."

"You look it," Anita said. "I wish I had enough hands to take a photo to email to Saber.

"I'll take one." At the front of their line, Rory pulled out his phone and snapped a shot before they could start a heated protest.

They scampered around the corner and broke contact.

Edwina focused on Rory. "Let us see."

He extended his phone, and Suzie groaned. "It's as bad as I feared, but it's not silly to send a couple of action shots home. Snap more and send them to London for the social media page."

"You have social media pages?" Rory asked, his shock evident. "What about humans?"

"We have a private forum for the local shifters. The Feline Council runs it, and they approve who can and can't have access, but we have a public page where we post photos of local events and news. We all have human friends, and we told them we were coming to Scotland for an exchange program," Suzie explained. "They'll be expecting photos."

"There's a fountain. Ah, other groups have the same idea," Rory said. "We should hustle."

They broke into an easy jog and headed for the fountain. Once closer, Anita spotted a yellow paper taped on the side. A petite bird shifter plucked it away and joined her group before Anita could speak.

Rory had seen too. "Check the fountain base for more clues."

Anita circled the fountain—a Grecian woman with an urn. Water arced from the top of the pot to land in a pool at her feet.

"Found one," Edwina shouted, triumph in her tone.

Anita and Rory huddled with Edwina and Suzy to read the clue.

"A non-venomous snake that is helpful with water. Any clues?" Edwina asked.

"They would hardly attach a clue to a snake," Suzy pointed out. "So it's a metaphor of some type."

"Let's walk and talk," Rory said.

Anita pondered this and spotted a gardener dressed in a green uniform. He was deadheading flowers. "How do they water the plants here? An underground irrigation system, or do they go old school with a hose?"

"There's a garden shed over there near that gardener," Suzie said. "Perhaps we can ask him."

Before they could act on the suggestion, another gardener appeared. They had a quick discussion before downing tools and retreating.

"It must be their break," Rory said. "Let's check around the shed, anyway."

"The other teams have disappeared," Anita said.

Rory shrugged. "Doesn't mean we're wrong. They might have received a different clue."

They jogged around a corner, their pace increasing on spotting a neatly coiled hose.

"We were right," Suzie said, her excitement contagious. She tugged at a bright yellow slip of paper. "If I were nasty, I'd take all the clues, but we want to win fair and square."

Heads together, they scanned the new clue.

"That's easy," Anita said. "I passed a memorial stone on the loch track. It's a memorial to a laird's favorite hunting dog."

"Let's go," Rory said. "I know the spot you mean. You lead the way, Anita."

"He wants to watch your butt," Suzie said.

"True," Rory replied without hesitation. "But it's better for one of you to set the pace since we have to finish the hunt together."

Anita grinned as she moved off in the lead. She felt the weight of a gaze, and her smile widened. The knowledge Rory wanted to watch her had her pulse racing and her thoughts sliding toward lovemaking. She led Rory and her friends past a rose garden, the bushes bearing pale pink flowers. The sweet floral scent filled the air until they were clear and entering the coolness of the trees. Sharp, refreshing pine tinged each breath, and dried needles and leaves crackled underfoot.

Anita turned right to follow the path snaking through the trees. The track was a gentle incline, and she leaned forward, propelling herself up the hill. Without warning, something punched into her shoulder. She tripped and vaguely heard a crack of sound as she struck the ground.

Chapter 18

Danger

"Anita!" Adrenaline fueled Rory as he scooped her off the path and slid behind a tree.

A second shot echoed around them, the bark of sound, followed by silence, had the hair rising at his nape.

Edwina popped from behind a leafy bush. "Is someone shooting at us?"

"Stay down." Rory turned Anita in his arms, his hands trembling as he fumbled to check for injuries. The tang of blood propelled him to greater haste.

Suzie poked her head from behind a tree, and a third shot broke the forest silence.

"Stay behind the tree," Rory snapped.

"Is she all right?" Edwina asked. "She's bleeding."

"Anita!" Rory feared his heart might beat out of his chest. Blood bloomed on her right shoulder, turning her blouse red. He pulled the fabric aside and lifted her slightly to check her back. "It looks like the bullet traveled straight through. Let's get her back to the castle medics." He ripped Anita's blouse and used the cloth as a pad to staunch the blood flow.

"Rory?" Anita's eyes fluttered. She shifted a fraction and groaned. "What happened?"

"Someone shot you," Rory said. "They're still firing." He peeked from where he and Anita sheltered. Seconds later, another report echoed around them. A bullet struck the tree trunk inches above Rory's head, and a piece of bark flew, hitting his cheek.

"They have us pinned down," Suzie said. "What are we going to do? We need to get Anita checked out."

Voices sounded in the distance—the loud chatter of a group. The gunman would either shoot at them or retreat. When nothing happened and the conversation grew closer, Rory risked another glance from behind the tree. He caught a flash of dark green moving through the undergrowth above them but couldn't hear anything. The voices increased in number, and Rory stood. He was in clear sight now, should the gunman care to shoot him.

Nothing happened.

Rory's legs shook, but he stood strong and scooped Anita into his arms. "Let's go."

"Anita, how are you doing?" Suzie asked.

The approaching groups of shifters stood aside, no doubt smelling the blood.

"Do you require help?" a skinny man asked.

"Someone shot at us," Edwina said. "We think they're gone, but take care."

"Gunfire?" a woman asked.

"Our friend has the hole in her to prove it." Edwina snapped and hurried after Rory. "Imbeciles. Did they not hear the shots? Some people are born stupid."

"What if the shooter has gone ahead?" Suzie asked.

Rory set a rapid pace, and the open ground between the castle and the forest lay before them. "We'll have to risk it. I'll up my pace, and if the shooter fires, we'll dodge and weave and pray for the best."

"I'll run ahead and get help. The presence of other shifters halted the shooter," Suzie said.

"Be careful," Anita said in a strained voice. "I'd hate for anyone to get hurt because of me."

Suzie darted past and sprinted into the open. Rory took several hasty steps and burst out of the forest.

Despite their fears, nothing happened.

When they ran up the front steps, Suzie had already spoken with the steward, and he'd summoned aid. A medic arrived, a large, no-nonsense woman with her two assistants. Rory started after them, not wanting to let Anita out of his sight. Despite Rory's protests and his wolf's growls, they carted Anita away.

Angus, the steward, stepped in front of them. "Come this way. It will be quieter in my office." Despite Rory's dissenting snarl, Angus ushered them down a passage and into an office. Everything inside sat in precise neatness, much like the steward's appearance. "Take a chair."

Rory let Edwina and Suzie shuffle past him and sit before he sank into the remaining chair. The steward stepped behind his desk.

"Tell me what happened." His gaze ran over each of them and lingered on Rory's bloodstained shirt.

"We were doing the treasure hunt," Rory said. "Suzie and Edwina were part of our team, along with Anita. We'd discovered our first two clues and were on the way to where we thought we'd find our next. We were running along the forest path, with Anita in the lead and me behind her. Edwina and Suzie followed me. We noticed nothing odd nor spotted strangers around until Anita fell. Then we heard the gunshot. I grabbed Anita and took cover.

The gunman continued firing whenever we peeked out and kept that up until we heard voices. Two other teams approached us on the same track. I caught a flash of green—a man—when I scanned our surroundings. When other shifters appeared, it was clear the gunman had left, so we hustled back with Anita."

Rory glanced at Edwina and Suzie. They seemed as mystified as him.

"This gentleman saw a person wearing green clothing. Did you see anything? Do you have comments to add?" the steward asked.

"I saw a figure wearing green," Edwina said. "It was the same color as the gardener's green uniform shirts."

The steward's eyes narrowed. "Our gardeners don't wear green. They don't have a specific uniform."

"When we were looking for our second clue, we saw two men. They wore green shirts, and it looked as if they were deadheading the roses. When we approached the shed, they set down their tools and left. We noticed because we intended to question them, hoping they could help us," Suzie said.

Angus scowled. "Describe these men."

Edwina shook her head. "One had black hair and the other brown. Their bodies seemed fit and strong, and they wore the same green shirts. I saw little more than this. Did you?"

"No," Rory agreed. "I didn't even register their hair color. I saw their uniforms. The pair were working with plants, and I assumed they were gardeners."

"You saw nothing while you were walking on the track?" the steward asked.

"No, not until Anita fell," Edwina said.

Rory stood. "I'd like to check on Anita."

The steward frowned. "I don't like this. We have security, and this shouldn't have happened. I'd suggest you don't go outdoors or wander alone. I will question the security team and increase our patrols. Do you think your friend saw anything?"

Rory shook his head. "I'll ask her, but we were hustling and not expecting problems. We were aware of our surroundings, but the gunfire surprised us. There were no strange scents to warn us of problems."

"Which means they shot your friend from a distance," the steward said thoughtfully. "Have you had trouble during your stay? Before you arrived at the castle?"

"No," Rory said. "Nothing to make someone shoot at me."

"What about Ms. Gatto?"

"She's from New Zealand. I doubt someone would follow her here to shoot her."

"What about any problems this week?"

"I've spent most of this week with Anita. If she hasn't been with me or in her room, she's spent time with her friends. I doubt anyone would want to hurt her. She's a pleasant woman." *Nice understatement.* He and his wolf wanted her with every fathom of their being. She was their other half, even if she didn't wear their mark on her shoulder. "Can I leave to check on Anita?"

Angus picked up a pen and tapped his desk. "Please stay within the castle and its immediate grounds. It's best not to put yourself at risk."

Rory pressed his lips together but didn't release the retort tingling at the tip of his tongue. He needed to learn if Hugh had left when he'd ordered him or if the team had followed Rory's grandmother's orders and stayed to monitor him. His next task after he reassured himself Anita was okay. "Which way are the doctor's rooms?"

"Turn left out the door. The doctor has a surgery at the end of the passage," Angus said. "The medic would've taken her there."

Rory paused in the doorway. "Will you let me know if you learn anything?"

"Aye," Angus said. "When we find the shooter, they will receive punishment. I will not have a rogue gunman ruining this gathering's reputation."

"Thank you." Rory left and strode along the tiled corridor. A discreet sign on a wooden door said *Doctor's Office*. Rory knocked and opened the door, and followed his senses to the right. His first breath dragged in Anita's floral perfume, along with coppery blood. On entering the examination room, he found Anita lying on a medical couch. Her eyes were closed, and her face paler than usual. A white bandage wrapped around her upper chest. Behind him, Edwina and Suzie spoke in quiet voices to the doctor—a bespectacled young man with a foxy scent.

"How is she?" Rory asked, walking straight to Anita. He ached for physical contact and ran his fingertips along her arm. The relief was instantaneous, and when she raised a hand and allowed him to lace their fingers together, his wolf hummed approval.

Anita's eyelids fluttered, and she opened her beautiful brown eyes. "I'm fine. Sore, but my feline has healed the worst of the injury."

The doctor crossed the room to stand beside Rory. "She'll be sore and bruised for a day or two. She's strong and healthy, and I don't foresee any complications. I cleaned the wound, and that probably caused more pain than the actual injury."

"Can I take her back to her room?"

"Aye, but if Anita develops symptoms or runs a temperature, call me. I'll check on her later this evening. She should take it easy and rest."

"Thank you, Doctor," Rory said, the pressure on his chest easing now that Anita was awake.

"I'll call a servant to help you to your room," the doctor said.

"I'll carry her." Rory pulled a face. "Sorry, my wolf is volatile at present. He's having a hard enough time knowing you've touched Anita. Another male mightn't fare so well."

The doctor offered a rueful smile. "Thank you for not biting off my head."

"You treated her, and I can sense you want her to recover," Rory said.

"You're welcome. I doubt infection will be an issue, but if the wound becomes red around the edges or gives Anita any problems, please call me."

"We will," Rory said. "Edwina, could you get the door for me, please? Lass, I'll try not to jostle you."

"It's okay. I just want to sleep."

"That's the painkillers I gave her," the doctor said. "They'll make her sleepy. Rest is the best cure. It will speed her recovery."

"Thanks, Doc," Anita said.

Rory scooped her off the medical bed and tried hard not to hurt her. Her swift intake of breath told him he hadn't quite managed, but she didn't complain. Rory strode down the passage and up a set of stairs. He passed three suits of armor and several large paintings of ancestors with snooty expressions. Greek statues and other intriguing items sat in alcoves.

Edwina and Suzie hustled behind him, darting forward to open doors when necessary.

"We need a quick strategy meeting," Suzie said. "Someone deliberately shot at us. Who was his target?"

"Agreed," Rory said.

"We should ask the guys to come," Edwina said. "I haven't seen any of them today. Have you?"

"Ramsay isn't answering his phone," Anita said in a tired voice. "I haven't seen Scott or Liam."

"They may have met someone," Suzie said. "We promised each other we'd share details, but if it's early in the piece, they might have nothing to tell us yet." She winked at Anita. "You didn't share. Care to enlighten us as to why?"

"No."

"We're mates," Rory said at the same time. "*We're mates*," he repeated when Anita grimaced. "The only reason I haven't officially marked you is we need to settle the past. We need to talk."

"Ooh, secrets. A scandalous history." Edwina clapped her hands. "Where's the popcorn?"

"No," Anita said.

"No," Rory agreed.

"Aw, you're no fun," Edwina said.

Suzie laughed. "Let's leave these two to sort themselves out and find ourselves some mischief. Anita has our number if she needs us. Is it okay to leave you alone with this growling, posturing wolf?"

Anita gave a half-laugh that turned into a groan, and Rory ushered the two grinning women from Anita's room.

"You have my protection," he said in a quiet voice. "You're Anita's friends, which means you're my friends."

"Thanks," Suzie said.

Edwina scrutinized his face. "You mean it."

"I do. Anita will be a huge part of my life if I have my way. Hopefully, her friends will become mine." Rory meant every word, but he comprehended something else. He and his wolf would walk away from everything they knew and their beloved Highlands if it meant they could keep Anita in their life.

Chapter 19

Standing For His Mate

After Suzie and Edwina left, Rory helped Anita into bed.

"Do you need anything? Something to drink? Eat?" Rory asked.

"I'd love to have a shower, but I want to sleep more."

"I'll help you shower later."

"Can you help me take off my pants? The shirt is past saving, so rip or cut that away. I'd appreciate it." Anita sounded exhausted.

Rory made quick work of her request and tucked her into bed. In five minutes, she was sound asleep.

Rory debated if he had time to grab a clean set of clothes and his phone from his room. The first job on his agenda was to locate Hugh. He couldn't conceive of Hugh or his men taking a potshot at Anita, but he needed to question his fellow wolves.

After considering the shooting, he'd decided the shooter had wanted to scare them. He could've waited until Rory, Anita, and the girls were close enough for a kill shot. The shooter hadn't.

Until now, Rory had reacted instead of applying logic. The shooter was either lucky he'd hit Anita or very skilled and issuing a warning. Rory would bet on the second. There was an ex-soldier who'd specialized as a sniper in their pack...

Rory growled under his breath, his muscles quivering, and the anger, the fury, didn't come from solely his wolf. He hated this situation. He wanted to eradicate the unknown threat, but he'd need to investigate. Aye, cunning and careful examination first, then he'd take action.

After a quick check of Anita, he took possession of Anita's room key and left. He'd shower and check his messages before he returned to watch over his mate.

His room was empty when he arrived. Hugh's clothes still hung in the wardrobe, and his toiletries sat on the shelves in the en suite. Rory grabbed his phone from where he'd left it on the nightstand. He powered it on and pulled a face at the twenty missed calls. He sucked in a deep breath and listened to his voicemail.

The messages were from his increasingly shrill grandmother, the gist being that she hadn't sent him to the gathering to have an affair with a sly cat.

"Meet the she-wolves and make your choice. The pack future depends on you having children. A wolf of Henderson blood has always headed the pack, and that will change over my dead body."

Rory winced at the slam of the phone in his ear. That had been the last message. He checked his texts—most from his grandmother and two from customers wishing to learn the status of their orders. He fired off texts to Marcus and asked him to contact the customers with progress reports. That done, he began his search for Hugh.

Hugh answered on the first ring. "Problem?"

Rory rolled his eyes. "Where were you this morning?"

"Since you didn't need us, I used the opportunity to take the men on a training run. Angus told me about a running group and arranged for us to join them. We're at the pub in town having a well-earned beer and lunch."

"What time did you leave?" Rory asked, even though he never doubted Hugh was telling the truth. His reply was unhesitating and simple enough for Rory to check.

"We left at seven-thirty to meet with the group in town. Why the questions?"

"I accompanied Anita and her two friends on a treasure hunt this morning. Someone shot Anita while we ran along the forest track."

Hugh cursed under his breath. "Is the lass all right?"

"She will be, according to the doctor. But the thing is, someone shot her from afar. I don't understand why the shooter didn't wait until we were closer."

"A sniper." Hugh's voice held tension.

"Aye, that's the way I'm thinking."

"Your grandmother is pissed," Hugh said. "She ordered me to watch you and make sure I kept you away from non-wolf shifters."

"And did you?"

"No." Hugh paused. "After you told me to leave you and return home, I started thinking. You're right. You're an adult and old enough to make your own decisions, and Elizabeth is attempting to control you. I wouldn't like it, so I understand why you're rebelling and ignoring her counsel."

"Can you ask your men if they've seen anyone loitering around the place?"

"Sure. Just a sec."

Rory heard Hugh give a succinct explanation and ask his questions. No one had noticed anything.

"We're heading back and will scout around the place. Describe the location where Anita got hit."

Rory outlined the portion of the track, feeling better, more confident now that he'd ascertained Hugh and the men had been nowhere near the forest. "Thanks. I'll be with Anita if you need me." Rory disconnected. A marksman—a skilled marksman—had made that shot. But why would they hit to injure instead of kill? That was the part he struggled with in this scenario. Was Anita the intended victim, or had it been him?

Not a single answer made sense.

Rory showered and changed clothes before seizing his phone. He had a couple of calls to make before he checked on Anita.

First, he rang Marcus. His friend noticed things. He'd tell Rory if anything out of the ordinary was bubbling with the pack.

"Hey, Marcus," Rory said when his friend grunted a hello.

"Rory." Marcus's tone changed from impatience to more laid back. "How's it going at the gathering?"

Rory hesitated before running with the truth. Marcus wouldn't blab information to Rory's grandmother. Elizabeth Henderson had never approved of their friendship, but Rory had continued to defy her from a young age and maintained their close friendship since they had so much in common. "I've met someone," he said. "A woman whose family used to work for the pack."

"Aye?" The word emerged as a question, prompting Rory to continue.

"Anita Gatto. Her parents are Ross and Blair Lennox. Do you remember them?"

"Aye, the gillie. His wife worked in the castle. I vaguely recall their daughter. She was younger than us, but didn't they leave for a better job in England?"

"No," Rory said. "My grandmother forced them to leave after Anita approached us during a meal and told everyone she was my mate."

"What? You never told me this," Marcus said, and Rory could tell he had his friend's full attention now.

"My memory," Rory said, shaking his head. "I recall none of the events in Anita's story. Perhaps a vague recollection of her parents, but not much else."

"Did you ask Hugh?"

"He shut down and told me to ask my grandmother."

"Ugh," Marcus said.

"Yeah."

"Are you sure this Anita isn't lying?"

"If that was true, why wouldn't Hugh tell me she was lying? My gut says Grandmother has either threatened or blackmailed everyone to keep quiet."

"Is this woman your mate?"

"Aye. I have not a single doubt. I haven't marked Anita yet, but I will. Someone shot her this morning."

"What the fuck?" Marcus muttered.

"The doctor says she'll make a full recovery, but I'm not positive if I was the target or Anita."

"Want me to nose around and see if I learn anything?"

"Aye, but don't put yourself in Grandmother's way. I'm not there to save your skin."

Marcus snorted. "You've made life bearable and improved life for every pack member. If it weren't for you, I would've moved my parents elsewhere and started afresh with another pack. My mother's pack would welcome us."

"Aye, Marcus. I know." Rory hesitated before telling Marcus more. "Anita came with a group of felines from New Zealand. We haven't discussed it, but I get the impression she isn't keen on relocating to the Highlands. If I want her, I'll have to live in New Zealand."

Marcus was silent for a moment. "You're thinking about it."

"Aye."

"If you decide to leave, you'll give me a heads-up? My parents considered leaving several years ago, but life improved once you took over."

"If you have time, research the town of Middlemarch in the South Island of New Zealand. Anita's so enthusiastic about the community, but it wouldn't hurt to investigate from a wolf standpoint."

"What if I ask Rowena to help with that part? I could keep the details general and say we're thinking about a business opportunity and you'd like background before you take the discussions further."

"Tell her to keep it on the down-low," Rory warned. "I don't want this getting back to my grandmother before I'm ready to act."

"Your grandmother isn't here. She left yesterday with a retinue of guards and hasn't returned."

Rory stiffened at this news. "Are you positive you didn't miss seeing her return?"

"Everyone appears relaxed. When your grandmother takes charge, the wolves become tense."

Rory pulled a face because he understood Marcus's meaning. His grandmother possessed an uncertain temper. Staff knew to tread warily when she was in one of her moods.

"All right. Take care, Marcus. My wolf is uneasy, and I'm not sure if it's because of Anita's injuries or it's something else."

"How's the sex?" Marcus asked, laughter in his voice.

"Mind your business," Rory said without heat.

Marcus chuckled and hung up.

Rory smiled. The sex was incredible, and once he'd marked her, it'd become spectacular, but he couldn't will away the nagging feeling assailing him. This oasis with Anita felt like the calm before a vicious storm, and he had no idea from which direction trouble might strike.

Chapter 20

Terror From The North

A quick tap on the door announced Rory's arrival. Anita sniffed and frowned when she didn't register his scent.

"What's wrong?" Edwina asked.

Suzie had gone to get them something to eat.

"I can't scent—" Anita broke off when the door flew open. A gasp escaped, and terror turned her limbs to ice.

"Who are you?" Edwina asked. "You've got the wrong room."

"Get her out," Elizabeth Henderson ordered the four bulky kilt-wearing men who accompanied her.

They manhandled Edwina out of Anita's bedroom and were none too gentle about it. Edwina fought them every step of the way, but eventually, they shoved her into the passage.

"Get out," Elizabeth said to her men.

The beefy Scots glided from the room, the door clicking shut behind them. Anita's senses told her they'd stopped outside in the passage, no doubt awaiting Elizabeth Henderson's further instructions.

After her initial surge of terror, Anita inhaled a deep breath and let it ease out. If she let this woman push her around again, she'd never forgive herself. She wasn't a raw teenager, and she didn't have to bow to bullies.

"I told you what would happen if you came near my grandson again."

Yep, in excruciating detail. Now bitter memories rushed back to thump Anita over the head.

Anita met the woman's stony gaze without flinching. Elizabeth had aged well, and her face bore few wrinkles. Her dark brown hair held the same red highlights as Rory's, but Elizabeth had ice-blue eyes. She was tall for a woman and kept herself fit. She'd acquit herself well in a fight, but she mostly used others to do her dirty work.

"You promised not to approach Rory. I had to show you I wasn't bluffing. You have one last chance to leave Scotland and never return. Insist on remaining, and the next shot will go through your heart. The following through your skull. You might be a shifter, but I doubt you'd survive a head shot."

Anita sat up straighter and ignored the pain in her upper chest. "You arranged the shooter."

There was a kerfuffle in the passage, and Elizabeth frowned. The bedroom door flew open, and Rory strode inside with Edwina, Suzie, and another wolf she'd seen around with Rory. Anita thought his name was Hugh.

Rory planted his hands on his hips. "Grandmother, what are you doing here?"

"You weren't answering my calls."

"And yet I find you in Anita's bedroom with your security team standing watch at the door. If you wished to talk to me, shouldn't you have sought me rather than Anita?"

Anita studied the older woman and watched her jaw clench. This meeting wasn't going the way she'd planned, and she despised losing control.

"Anita tells me you booted her and her family from their job with the pack." Rory's voice was mild, but his features were cold.

Elizabeth sniffed. "I assure you the Lennox family left our pack of their own accord."

"Lie," Rory said.

Elizabeth wheeled and turned her ice-blue glare on Anita. "What has she been telling you? Why would you listen to her rather than your own blood?"

"Anita is my mate," Rory said.

Elizabeth drew a sharp breath, and her glower increased. "She is a cat. You would dilute our bloodlines and cleave yourself to a dirty, lowbred feline?"

"Aye," Rory said. "She is my true mate, and my loyalty is to her."

"What about your pack? They'd never accept a flea-ridden feline."

"Hey, who are you calling flea-ridden?" Suzie demanded.

"The pack doesn't need to accept my mate. What happens in the future is between Anita and me. No one else. Grandmother, tell me the truth. What did you do back then? Why don't I remember?"

Hugh's jaw set, his focus on Elizabeth determined. "He deserves the truth."

Elizabeth sniffed. "I have nothing to say."

"Your grandmother threatened me." Anita bore no loyalty to the woman. "She orchestrated the shooting this morning and advised she'd make sure the next bullet drilled my heart or head. Elizabeth informed me this was my last warning."

Rory noticeably flexed his fingers, not removing his focus from his grandmother. "Anita is my mate. Nothing will change the truth. Threatening her won't do you any favors."

Elizabeth cursed. Several vicious Anglo-Saxon expletives turned the air blue. "What about your loyalty to your pack? You owe them. They require security and for the pack to remain pure."

Rory's snort echoed through the bedroom. "This modern world comes with challenges. The old ways no longer work, and we must become flexible."

Elizabeth ignored Rory's comment and sneered at Anita. "You shouldn't have returned to Scotland. You should've stayed in that isolated little town with your filthy brethren."

Anita released a hiss. "I didn't know Rory was coming to the gathering. For all I knew, he had married and had six children. I tried to avoid him and keep to our pact, but Rory is determined."

"Which is why I had to take action," Elizabeth snapped. "I can't let you enter our pack."

"Who would want to join your pack?" Suzie demanded. "You're not smiling and bringing out an enthusiastic welcome."

"No one asked you. This is none of your business."

"Grandmother, what did you do back then?"

"I don't know what you mean."

But Anita caught the rapid flicker of her eyes before Elizabeth controlled her body language. Anger flooded Anita, but she forced it back. Best to use her words rather than her fists. Beating up an older woman wouldn't win Anita points, even if the wolf was a conniving bitch. This grannie forced her parents from a secure position and caused a rift in their family. Anita still felt guilty because her father had loved his job. It had been his passion, and Anita's actions had stolen that from him. Thankfully, her parents enjoyed their new life with its continental excitement and challenges. But in between had been challenging with depression and hardship. She would never forgive Elizabeth Henderson for inflicting that suffering on her parents.

Hugh stepped forward. "I've had enough of the lies. All these years, I've kept your secrets because I believed you told me the truth. As a child, I saw the damage the feline clan did to your family, and I was glad when our pack drove them from the Highlands. Elizabeth, like you, I saw Rory as the future of our pack and believed we needed a she-wolf at his side for the pack to prosper. Rory has ignored every woman you've set in his way because, on some level, his wolf remembered he had a mate. Now, through a twist of fate, they've discovered each other again."

"It's a setup." Elizabeth sneered. "That cat did her research and inserted herself into Rory's path."

"No," Hugh said before Anita could stand up for herself. "I recognized her straightaway. It was her scent. It's distinctive. Anita still tilts her head when considering a matter. She was shocked to see Rory, and to her credit, she tried to stay away from him. Once Rory spotted her, he wasn't interested in anyone else. It was her he wanted, even though she kept trying to avoid him. He made sure he was close to her, and she continued to fight while he wore down her defenses."

Elizabeth snorted, her icy gaze flashing contempt at Anita. This woman refused to bend—that was clear. Anita might admit Rory was her mate, but his grandmother would never accept her. The wolf pack would suffer and split into factions—those who supported Elizabeth and those who followed Rory.

Anita closed her eyes, exhausted by the situation.

"Grandmother," Rory's voice held steel and an underlying power that had Anita's eyes opening. He'd never released his alpha power with her, but now he compelled obedience. "Grandmother," Rory repeated himself, the command in it snapping every wolf in the room to attention.

"Aye." The reply hissed through Elizabeth's clenched teeth. Her shoulders were straight, and she stood tall. Her gaze connected with Anita's, and it was full of disdain. Loathing.

Anita refused to glance away. No longer was she a young, untried feline. She didn't need to prove a thing since she'd survived two stepchildren and created a new life for herself.

As if he could read her strident thoughts, Rory stepped closer and picked up her hand. He squeezed lightly.

"Grandmother, why don't I recall Anita declaring herself my mate?"

Exactly what Anita wanted to learn. At first, she'd thought Rory had been lying, but he'd never slipped once nor betrayed knowledge of the event. Hugh had been a witness.

Elizabeth pressed her lips together and lifted her head. "I ran off an upstart cat who had ideas of infiltrating the pack and making us a laughingstock. Rory, if you insist on taking this woman as your mate, you're not welcome at the castle. Don't come home because I shall bar the castle gates."

Anita felt Rory's jolt of shock and barely re-strained her gasp at Elizabeth's effrontery since Rory was the alpha and in charge.

Elizabeth slid a mocking glance at Anita. "You will never rule at Castle Henderson while I have breath in my body. Enter, and danger will follow you. You'll need eyes in the back of your head to stay alive." On that declaration, she sailed to the door every inch the Highland queen.

There was a shocked instant when everyone in Anita's room stared after the departing wolf.

"Rory, you can't leave things this way with your grandmother. You can't lose your home because of me."

Rory didn't reply but stared at the open door.

The guards who had arrived with Rory's grandmother trailed her down the passage. Hugh and his team remained.

Hugh cleared his throat. "Rory, I'll tell ye. It will cost me because your grandmother is a stubborn and unbending woman. She'll not change her mind, but ye deserve the truth."

Chapter 21

Truth

Rory cursed, stunned at his grandmother's pronouncement. Despite his position as alpha, she was stepping up to challenge him rather than accepting his choice of mate. His lips twisted because he understood the way his grandmother worked. She would've considered the angles and expected him to come to heel.

He'd always seen situations from her point of view before. That'd be what she was anticipating. Not for the first time this week, he wished he'd thrown around his weight and forced his grandmother to follow his instructions.

But that was a moot point.

He hadn't because he loved the woman, and she'd taught him how to lead. The one thing he'd done in opposition to her wishes was training those who wanted to learn a woodworking trade. She'd conceded this hobby of his had brought funds to the pack, allowed them to make improvements at the castle, so they'd continued with furniture making.

He glanced at Anita and discovered her watching him. A sliver of fear flashed over her before her expression shuttered. Rory nodded at Hugh.

"I'd appreciate knowing the truth. Anita has told me bits and pieces, but I don't remember anything. Hell, I should remember my mate. My grandmother and I have treated Anita and her family shamefully, yet the entire event is like a black hole. To move on, Anita and I need to confront the problem."

Rory sat beside Anita.

"Should we stay?" Edwina asked, indicating Suzie and herself.

"Stay," Rory said. "You're Anita's friends. I trust you." The truth, he realized. He trusted Anita and her Middlemarch friends. Their loyalty to each other impressed him since it was a quality his pack lacked. He kicked himself for not seeing this earlier. His chest ached, and he felt torn. He couldn't lose Anita—not after he'd found her again. No matter what Hugh told him, he didn't intend to walk away. His wolf whined, the reaction unusual but understandable.

Castle Henderson was their home, their place of safety and happiness.

Hugh cleared his throat and spoke, jolting Rory from his tumultuous thoughts.

"Everything Anita told you is true," Hugh said. "Or at least from the snippets I've gathered, the things she mentioned to you are fact. During a family dinner, she stalked into the Great Hall and told everyone present you and she were mates."

Rory frowned, trying to recall the moment. He'd been there. He'd spoken to Anita, yet this vital occasion was a yawning black chasm. "What did I say?"

"You appeared as shocked as everyone else. You sat in your chair and stared at Anita." Hugh shook his head. "She was such a tiny thing. She focused entirely on you, and her eyes glowed a golden brown. It was your feline, I think. Elizabeth towered over her and glared down at Anita. Back then, those important to the pack sat on a raised dais. Anyway, Elizabeth blasted you with her power since she was the alpha. She snarled that Anita was mistaken, and Rory was not your mate. You were a deluded child with mental problems and not worthy of wiping Rory's shoes."

"Ah, yes," Anita murmured. "I'd forgotten that part."

Her careful voice hid none of her hurt and disillusionment, still present all these years later. The moment had been traumatic and life-changing for her and her family.

"Go on," Rory said to Hugh.

"Your grandmother instructed two of her security team to escort Anita home and to make certain you stayed there. She told Anita she'd be there later in the afternoon to speak to her parents."

Anita gave an audible swallow. "What happened after I left? I thought Rory was lying or playing me, but it's obvious he truly doesn't know what happened."

"I'm getting to that," Hugh said. "After the men escorted you from the Great Hall, Elizabeth turned to you, Rory. She demanded to know if you had encouraged the girl. From what I witnessed, you seldom saw Anita. Your paths didn't cross because Rory is older, but you informed your grandmother you liked her. Then you accused Elizabeth of rudeness, told her she was mean, and Anita wasn't to blame. Everyone witnessed your anger. You informed your grandmother you'd make things right, and you stood, intent on following Anita. That was when your grandmother lost the plot. She picked up a heavy serving plate, and when you walked past her, she struck you over the head. You toppled like a mighty oak and hit your head on the wooden table when you fell.

"Everyone stared, shocked by her actions. She stalked off, leaving you lying on the floor. You were out cold and unresponsive, with a pool of blood around your head. I called the medic, and we took you to your chamber. Everyone thought you'd die. You were unconscious for eight days, and when you stirred, you had no memory of the events. Elizabeth had made sure Anita left the castle and promised dire consequences to the family should they return. She also made certain everyone at the meal remained silent. She put about the story someone attacked you and surrounded you with bodyguards. Elizabeth scared everyone, and given the lack of compassion she'd shown Anita's family and also Rory, each of us understood our lives and those of our families were in danger should we speak a word of the truth."

"Remember when I fell off my horse and took a knock to the head? Grandmother had my horse destroyed." The knot in Rory's throat refused to leave while devastation twisted everything together. "I begged her not to, but she told me once a horse stepped out of line, it set a pattern of behavior."

"Aye," Hugh said, his voice grim. "That horse was the gentlest soul, but your grandmother didn't care. I think she feared another knock might bring back your memory. She wished her plot to succeed, and her relationship with you returned to normal. She allowed her hatred of the Highland felines who decimated her close family to rule her actions."

"Why did she hire Anita's parents if she hated felines so much?" Edwina asked.

"Elizabeth's late husband, Roland, hired them. Both Ross and Blair were excellent at their jobs and kept to themselves. They kept their heads down and didn't cause problems, so Elizabeth had no reason to single them out."

"Until I inserted myself into the pack," Anita said in a pained voice.

"Aye," Hugh agreed.

"Why are you telling me this now?" Rory asked.

"You and Anita could be happy together, and it's time to right the wrong."

"Grandmother won't let you return now," Rory said.

Hugh nodded. "I understand, but now that my parents have died, I have no one left for her to injure or make their lives difficult. I will leave and make a life elsewhere," he said.

"Promise you won't leave without telling me," Rory said.

"Aye." Hugh readily agreed.

"What about your men?" Anita asked.

"I'll speak with them, tell them the full story, and let them make up their minds," Hugh said. "Some like me don't enjoy woodworking but welcome other challenges."

"Why didn't you say?" Rory asked. "I hope I've been fair and approachable."

"You have, but your grandmother holds equal power, and our wolves fear her."

Shame stung Rory because, in hindsight, he could see this was true, and he'd failed as a leader. "Please don't leave without speaking to me." He dropped Anita's hand and stalked to the door, desperate to leave, to lick his wounds. He told himself he needed to think.

This was his fault.

If he'd spoken up, perhaps none of this would've happened. Hell, he was so confused, and he couldn't look at Anita. He'd mistreated her, and now he'd learned his entire pack had suffered under his grandmother. If he'd been a better leader, he would've stood up to her.

"Rory," Suzie's tone held disbelief.

He ignored her chastisement and closed the door after him, attracting the loitering bodyguards' attention. They would've heard everything, and Rory couldn't meet their gazes. He marched past and headed for the main entrance. He'd run and ponder how to make this up to Anita, his pack. His responsibilities weighed heavily on his shoulders. The hardest part would be facing his grandmother and exerting his will on her. If most of the pack feared her, that was no way to live a life. It was no wonder wolves were leaving.

Rory cursed long and loud, disgusted and full of self-loathing. He had to fix this mess. This injustice belonged to his pack, and as the alpha, he carried the majority of the guilt burden.

Chapter 22

Heartbreak

Anita stared after Rory, and the pain in her chest stole her breath. Was he leaving? Just like that?

The bodyguard cast her a sympathetic glance before exiting the room.

"The bastard," Edwina muttered. "How could Rory leave like that?"

"Maybe he's coming back," Suzie said.

"It doesn't matter," Anita said. "Us together wouldn't work. We want different things. He has his pack to look after while I want to return to New Zealand. It's my home now. I don't need a mate. I have friends in Middlemarch and through my job—shifter and human."

"You deserve better," Suzie snapped. "You have honor and integrity, and you're a good person. I didn't know you well before Saber picked us to attend the gathering, but I'm proud to call you a friend."

"Seconded," Edwina said.

"What are you going to do?" Suzie asked.

"I might fly to France and visit my parents. We're not close, but it'd be nice to see them. Then, I'll travel home."

"We'll come with you," Edwina said.

"No, stay and wave the flag for Middlemarch. Saber and London worked hard to persuade the rest of the Feline Council this gathering would benefit us. I'd hate to give the other council members ammunition to stop other shifters from receiving the opportunities we've had."

Suzie and Edwina shared a glance before the two friends turned back to her.

"You're right. Our grandmothers didn't want this. Saber and London fought for us," Edwina said.

Suzie nodded. "I admire our youngest Feline Council reps. They've been incredible and decent. They stood for us when we behaved like idiots and created trouble for everyone. We'll stay. How is your wound?"

Anita prodded the bandage with a ginger touch. "It's better. Not as painful. The flesh feels as if it has knitted together. I'll be fine by tomorrow. Why don't you join in the activities? I won't leave until tomorrow because I'll need to book a flight to France and try to change my one to New Zealand."

"Maybe Rory will come to his senses," Suzie suggested.

Edwina snorted. "And maybe Middlemarch felines will sprout wings and soar over the Southern Alps."

There was a brief pause until they broke into laughter.

"I'd pay to see that," Anita said with a companionable grin. The five Middlemarch shifters who'd come to Scotland with her had become a solid unit, and she didn't think that'd change once they returned home. One good thing that had come from the gathering.

A part of Anita hoped Rory might come to see her, but he'd left the castle before her. Anita sighed and strode into the local Middlemarch café—Storm in a Teacup—where she was meeting with Saber and London. The rest of her group wasn't due home from Scotland until the end of next week.

Tension and a strained welcome had greeted her when she'd visited her parents, but she felt happier and lighter now since she'd made an effort. She hadn't informed them about her recent meeting with Rory and had merely said she was in France on business and returning to New Zealand.

Saber and London were already waiting for her. The temperature had dropped with the promise of snow in the air. Anita had donned a woolen coat and a colorful scarf, even though she didn't suffer the cold as much as the typical human.

"You spent time in the sun, didn't you?" London said, peering at her.

"I did," Anita said. "Summertime in the Northern hemisphere, remember?"

"How did it go?" Saber asked, his intense green gaze searing through her. "You're home early."

"Yes."

Before Anita could speak, Emily, Saber's mate, arrived bearing a tray with a large pot of tea and three cheese scones fresh from the oven.

"Thanks, sweetheart," Saber said.

The doorbell dinged, and Emily muttered under her breath. "Bother, I wanted to eavesdrop."

Anita grinned at her disappointment while Saber pretended to glower at his wife.

"Why are you back early?" London asked.

Anita sighed and started talking. She told them about her early life in Scotland, her claiming Rory as her mate and her subsequent expulsion from the pack lands. She left nothing out and didn't make excuses.

"Wow," London said. "We wouldn't have sent you if we'd known your past would return to haunt you."

"It's okay," Anita said. "It wasn't all bad. Our group of six has become tight, and that's a plus. I'm sorry I failed." She paused before asking the question that burned her. "Do you think every shifter has several potential mates?"

"I don't know," Saber said. "I like to think we each have several possibilities, and it's about choices. Did the others discover a possibility?"

"Ramsay disappeared, and I hadn't seen him for a while. The guys told me they saw him briefly, so perhaps you might have more luck with him. Suzie and Edwina hadn't come across anyone interesting before I left."

"It doesn't matter," London assured her. "Finding a mate is a long shot. It was more about giving you experience with other shifters and the opportunity to learn and absorb ideas. It's better for us as a community if each of us grows."

Saber picked up a portion of scone and took a healthy bite. He chewed and swallowed. "What London said. Gathering attendance is an investment in our shifters and community."

"Despite the drama, I had fun," Anita said. "And I guess I've also put a lid on the past. I understand now why Rory never came after me or even demanded an explanation."

"Will you be okay?" London asked.

"Yeah, I'll be fine. I had a few hours' stopover in Paris and shopped in Dubai. That's definitely on the plus side. Getting shot—not so much."

Saber's brows drew together. "Did they catch the shooter?"

"Not that I know of, but Rory suspected it was one of his pack. An ex-army sniper. My impression was Elizabeth Henderson forced the man to shoot me. It would've been convenient if I'd died."

Saber drank his tea. "Have you checked in with Gavin?"

"I intend to," Anita said. "My shoulder is itchy, and it's driving me crazy."

"Was there anything else you needed to tell us?" Saber asked.

Anita thought back over the days and shook her head. "No, but I would like to thank you for sending me. As I mentioned earlier, now I have closure, I can move on."

Famous last words, Anita thought four hours later. Her feline was a mopey ball of fluff and full of the sulks. Anita had already deep-cleaned the kitchen and attacked the bathroom and toilet with the same vigor. No matter how hard she tried, her thoughts kept returning to Rory. She couldn't stop her pining, and even worse, she craved his touch.

After only a few days, she missed him. She'd shunted Rory Henderson to the past once, and she could do it again. There was no other alternative.

When Rory arrived at Castle Henderson and analyzed the current situation, he realized he'd been fooling himself. Placing his loyalty for his only remaining family ahead of the pack had resulted in these dire consequences. They were existing, and aye, they were doing well financially because he made sure everyone received equal shares of the wealth, but it wasn't enough. Stupidly, during his absence, he'd allowed his grandmother access to his accounts. A mistake since the nest egg he'd accumulated and invested was no longer in the bank.

Rory left the castle and climbed the hill to their main workshop.

"Marcus, what happened?" Numerous bruises in colors ranging from blue to purple and a few yellow covered his friend's face.

"Your grandmother's goons," Marcus said. "They planned their attack well and struck when I was the only one working."

"What did they want?"

"The safe key. I tried to tell the guards I didn't have it, and they'd have to wait until your return. Your grandmother appeared and told me she'd gut me if I didn't hand it over, but she'd start on the pups first. When I was slow to obey, she ordered her bodyguards to hack off Toby's right arm. They refused, so she did it herself."

"She what?" Rory asked in a hoarse voice.

Marcus swallowed hard. "Then she called for the next pup. She was laughing. God, Rory. I disliked your grandmother and considered her cruel, but I never thought her capable of this vindictiveness. Toby's parents heard the commotion and came running. The guards held them back, but when Oliver punched Elizabeth, she turned the broadsword on him. She killed Oliver and his wife without hesitation, and it was obvious she intended to keep her word because she ordered her men to line up every male pup. I surrendered the key."

"Where is she now?" Rory asked. "She's not at the castle."

Marcus swallowed hard. "She muttered something about arranging your wedding."

"Not going to happen unless it's to Anita," Rory said without hesitation. In that heartbeat, he understood what his wolf had tried to tell him during their homeward journey. Castle Henderson was no longer home because Anita wasn't here. "Where's Toby?"

"Albany took him to the medical team. We're hoping they can reattach his arm."

"I'm going to hunt down my grandmother," Rory said. "How many men does she have?"

"The usual four, but her behavior sickened them. That was easy to see. I don't think they'll protect her if she waves her sword around again." Marcus shook his head, tears welling in his eyes. He swiped them away. "It was as if she'd snapped. She kept talking to herself and cackling. A lot of the families have packed their things and left. I don't blame them. Honestly, I doubt I can stay now."

In that instant, Rory's decision was straightforward. Once he punished his grandmother and stopped her from damaging the pack any further, he'd leave and start over with Anita—if she'd have him.

Chapter 23

Alpha Business

Rory spent fruitless hours searching for his grandmother. When he couldn't locate her, he used his time to speak to his pack members. He ground his teeth together, sick-at-heart, his shoulders stiff from recalling each nasty verbal blow coming from the lips of wolves he'd known since he was a gangly pup. His wolf sizzled with fury, and a growl rolled up Rory's throat. He'd wished his people had felt they could tell him their problems with his grandmother. Now armed with the truth, it was simple to discern the she-wolves' uneasiness. The older wolves' discontent. He'd listened closely, then spoken to each wolf he encountered and told them of his plans. They were welcome to join him if they wished.

"Do ye wish to know our decisions now?" a male wolf slightly older than Rory asked.

"Nay. Discuss it with your mate, your parents, and grandparents. No matter what happens, I promise you'll have a roof over your head."

"Thank ye," the man said, his accent far broader than Rory's.

Rory made his way around everyone before trudging back to Castle Henderson. The weathered gray stone and the square watchtowers had never seemed welcoming or full of light like Castle Glenkirk, but it had been home. *Until now.* Today Rory took in the water-filled castle moat and the sole occupant of the guardhouse at the drawbridge.

"Is my grandmother at home?" he asked the tall, solid wolf who studied him with an impassive stare—another new employee.

His grandmother surrounded herself with these paid-for-hire men, which might prove a problem to him. Rory couldn't count on his pack to back him. He wasn't even confident of Hugh and his team.

"My grandmother?" Rory prompted when the wolf's lips twisted in disdain. That answered his question. This wolf held no loyalty to Rory. An enemy.

"She arrived back half an hour ago. She is in the Great Hall."

"Thank you," Rory murmured and stalked past, no longer displaying the disappointment and defeat that burdened him. Now was not the time to show his tender belly. His grandmother was forging ahead with her plans, and he had to stand up to her and let her know he disagreed with the future as she saw it.

Rory heard her first. She was screeching, which was never a great sign. Usually, Rory would detour and head for the woodwork workshop. Not today. He strode into the Great Hall, noting the occupants. Several heavy tables and chairs sat on either side of the room. The stark gray interior echoed the outside facade, with wall tapestries providing contrasting color. An enormous fireplace took up a portion of one wall, but the hearth was empty, a fire unnecessary during the height of summer.

"Ah," Elizabeth said on spotting him. "You're here. They said you were wandering the pack lands and visiting our wolves."

"I was, but now I'm here."

"This is Catriona, your future wife. Come here, lass, and meet your mate." Elizabeth grasped Catriona's arm and, given the girl's flinch, it was clear his grandmother was hurting her.

Irritation flooded Rory, but he didn't let it show or loosen the reins on his temper. Now was not the time. First, he needed to help the girl.

"Catriona," he said, holding out both hands for her to grasp.

Satisfaction swirled over his grandmother's face, and thankfully, she released the girl. Catriona didn't seem any happier to touch him, so he dropped his hands and smiled at her.

"Are you staying here tonight?"

"Of course, she is," his grandmother scoffed. "The minister will officiate, binding you legally in a human way and in that of pack law. Catriona's parents insisted on this. They will arrive in a few hours to witness your nuptials."

"I see," Rory said. His grandmother intended to make certain Anita remained out of his life.

"Catriona, I'm sure you'd like to rest and prepare," Rory said, never taking his focus off his grandmother. He still couldn't believe she'd killed Toby's parents and willfully injured Toby, an innocent pup. Rory had checked on Toby. Unfortunately, the medics hadn't managed to reattach his arm, but the boy was healing and would live. Rory's nostrils flared, and he struggled to hide his fury.

Elizabeth had murdered innocents simply because they'd wanted to protect their child. *Innocents.*

"Is there someone who could show Catriona to my chamber?" Rory asked.

When no one replied, Hugh stepped forward. "I will take you to the housekeeper." He offered his arm to Catriona and smiled when she gingerly placed her fingers on his sleeve.

Once Hugh and Catriona left, Rory turned to his grandmother. "I see you've been busy while I attended the gathering."

"The pack doesn't run on its own," his grandmother said.

"You required pack reserves to celebrate properly?" he asked in a mild voice.

She went still, her eyes narrowing a fraction. "The wedding of the pack alpha is a monumental event. We must celebrate in style."

"You injured Toby. Killed his parents. Why? They were blameless."

"They stood in the way of progress."

"Progress," Rory scoffed. "You ordered Marcus to hand over the key to the safe, and when he refused, you chopped off Toby's arm and killed his parents when they tried to intervene. That's not fuckin' growth. That's senseless murder."

Elizabeth sniffed. "Don't use that tone with me. I'm your grandmother and deserve your respect."

"*Respect?* Respect isn't commanded. You earn it, and you've done nothing to earn mine or the rest of the pack. My grandmother is a coward and a bully. You surround yourself with hired hitmen, and everyone in the pack is too frightened to stand against you."

Elizabeth lifted her nose into the air, unruffled by his accusations. The men standing around her—the paid wolves—stood straighter, each of them on alert.

The door behind Rory opened, and Hugh stepped inside. Several wolves followed him and arranged themselves in a semi-circle behind Rory. A breath eased out of Rory. He hadn't been certain his clansmen would support him after he'd failed them so badly.

"Hear this, Grandmother," Rory said. "I refuse to marry Catriona. Anita is my mate, and she is the only woman I will ever consider."

"I told you not to return if you were considering hooking yourself to that scruffy cat," Elizabeth snapped. "I can't let you do that."

"Try and stop me. No," he said when she signaled her hired assassins. "This is between you and me. You don't get others to do your dirty work. Stand down." His alpha power surged and washed through the Great Hall. It was fitting this encounter was here where everything with Anita had started.

Elizabeth's guards stood frozen, their mouths slack as they gaped at him. He'd never done this before, never wanted to force his people into following his orders. He'd never displayed his raw power to his grandmother either, and he caught the surge of interest in her face. The satisfaction. Despite his words, she thought she'd won because he was here and exerting his alpha power to get his way. He recalled his father telling him it was a heady ability and, if misused, it rotted the mind and character.

With his father's warning in mind, he'd used intelligence and reasonable persuasion in his decisions. He hadn't abused his power.

"Hugh, get me the ceremonial sword," he said without taking his gaze off his grandmother. Disgust filled him when her eyes widened, but he took no satisfaction from the fear that followed. This would be a fair fight, one fought on even ground. "It is my job as alpha of this pack to maintain the law. You murdered two innocent people and injured their son in a way that will affect his entire life. It was not up to you to mete out punishment."

Elizabeth's head lifted, and her power swirled around her.

Rory never blinked, and this made her frown. She'd underestimated him and had never considered he might take action against her. She thought him weak.

"You don't have witnesses."

"Ah, but you know that isn't true. I have a witness."

Elizabeth cursed and whirled to glare at the dazed wolves.

"Aye, they left Marcus bruised but very much alive."

"He's lying. What did he tell you?"

"He's not lying," Rory said evenly. "Toby told me the same tale. Elizabeth Henderson, you have committed a heinous crime against the pack, and your punishment is death."

Her facial muscles went slack before she drew herself up taller. It was apparent she didn't believe in Rory's determination.

"Do you wish to confess or fight to the death?" he asked.

"You wouldn't kill your kin. I'm your grandmother, Rory."

Rory stared at her, a roiling heat in his belly. "You have gone through life blaming everyone else instead of taking personal responsibility for your failures. Today I heard a dozen cases where you took what you wanted. Behind my back, you stole from our people. You treated them as nothing. For months, I've puzzled over why our wolves were leaving. It was desperation because they were too terrified to speak against you."

"Who has been telling tales?" she demanded, the haughty Highland Queen once again.

Hell, she still believed she could wriggle out of this. "Escort the hired wolves from the castle. Hugh, please pay them from my private funds and see them on their way."

Elizabeth reached out, and he stepped back. "You can't do this," she said, a note of pleading in her tone.

"Leave!" Rory thundered to Elizabeth's wolves.

They departed on soundless feet with no argument.

Rory stalked over to where the clan claymore sat atop a red velvet cloth. A second sat beside it. He plucked both out of the open case and closed the distance between him and Elizabeth. He'd make this a fair fight, but he was under no illusions. She'd fight dirty.

He hadn't seen it before, but he saw the corruption in her now. *It hurt*. Bile burned at the back of his throat. The hard thudding of his heart showed his increased heart rate. This sucked, but he understood what he needed to do to make everything right.

"Fight me," he ordered his grandmother. "We'll finish this the right way."

"You can't kill me." Her icy-blue eyes held fury. Smug confidence.

Rory held up his claymore in a defensive position and waited, his weight balanced evenly, his muscles relaxed.

Killing her was the right thing to do, and there was no turning back.

Chapter 24

Reunion

Middlemarch, New Zealand

"Anita, we've got a group of visitors arriving this afternoon," Saber said when Anita answered the phone. "I wondered if you could help London wrangle them. Emily is short-handed at the café. Agnes is sick, and Valerie is still visiting family in the North Island."

"No problem. What do you want me to do?" Anita asked, pleased to have a task. Any job to fill her mind instead of that thoughtless, self-centered, no-good wolf.

"Act as hostess and introduce the visitors to locals. We're starting at the town hall before we give them a tour of the area. We'll take a group tour each and finish at Storm in a Teacup. Emily might want you and London to serve food there."

"Happy to help. What time do you need me? Should I dress in anything special?"

"Wear your normal clothes," Saber said. "Meet us at the Town Hall at one."

When Anita arrived at one, voices rippled from inside the hall. She locked her car and walked to the entrance, a smile fixed on her lips. Mentally, she crossed her fingers and prayed she had the fortitude to keep the smile natural for the entire afternoon. Her phone rang.

"Hello?"

"Are you almost here?" Saber asked. "We're running early."

"I'm in the car park."

"Great." Saber hung up.

Anita inhaled and came to a screeching halt. *Wolf musk*. That wasn't unusual since they had three wolves in the area, but these scents indicated strangers.

"Anita."

Her eyes widened, and she fumbled her phone. She blinked hard, convinced her mind had conjured a mirage. She took two steps. Halted. "Rory?"

"Aye."

In that instant, she understood she'd been lying to herself. She'd desperately missed Rory and wasn't functioning without him. At least she'd pried herself from bed and had taken a shower and changed clothes. She'd stopped crying, but sleeping had become a problem. Now he was here...

Anita found herself running, sprinting across the uneven ground. She hurled herself at him, and his arms wrapped around her. His wild wolfish scent surrounded her, and everything wrong in her world clicked into the correct place. Their lips met, and they kissed hungrily. Finally, she pulled back and stared up at him.

"What are you doing here?"

"Home is where you are," he stated. "You're my mate, Anita. I'm only half a wolf without you."

"What about your grandmother?"

Rory's face twisted, and pain slashed across his features. "I'm not making excuses, but she wasn't well. Wild Highland felines attacked the pack and killed her family when she was a child. She and her mother received severe injuries. No one expected Grandmother to survive, but she recovered. She seemed fine until you declared you were my mate. She hated felines, and it was only my grandfather who persuaded her to give your parents a chance. When you insisted we were mates, memories played with her mind." He held up a hand. "Not an excuse. I'm merely explaining what happened. She got rid of you and your parents, and I didn't notice problems within the pack. When I attended the gathering and started paying attention to you, it snapped her mind. She murdered innocents. *Pack*." He swallowed, his voice turning bleak. "I had to execute her."

Anita stared at him, a wave of sympathy curling through her chest. She placed her hand on his shoulder. "I'm so sorry. That must've been horrid."

"None of this is your fault or mine. My grandmother was responsible."

"What about your pack?"

"While I was at the gathering, several families left to join relatives. I contacted Saber and asked him if there was room for wolves in Middlemarch—those who wanted a fresh start. He agreed, and twenty wolves came with me to New Zealand. Saber has found us accommodation and jobs and arranged the relevant visas. Those wolves who wished to stay did so with my blessing."

"That takes months. The visas, I mean."

"Saber told me one of his cousins works in the department and could fast-track the process."

Anita swallowed hard and met Rory's gaze. "You're truly staying?"

"Aye, if you'll have me."

"Yes." Anita didn't hesitate.

"Ah, there's one more thing. I hope you don't mind. Toby?"

A young boy burst out of the Town Hall and ran to Rory. One of his shirt sleeves flapped, and she realized the boy was missing part of an arm.

"My grandmother." Rory's voice held disgust and threaded with pain. "Toby has no close family left, and since my grandmother caused this, I have taken responsibility for him. He's a great kid and adjusting well."

"Hello, Toby. My name is Anita."

"Rory and I is gonna live with you," Toby said, cocking his head and sniffing loudly to gain her scent.

Anita smothered her grin. "Mr. Henderson, rather sure of yourself, aren't you?"

Rory slipped his arm around her waist. "More hopeful but determined to woo you until you accept our way of thinking. I understand the idea of another stepchild mightn't thrill you, but I can't abandon him. I can't."

"My house is big enough for Toby and a few more children."

Rory's features relaxed. "This is way more than I deserve. I still remember little of what happened when you first claimed me."

"It doesn't matter. We'll count the gathering as the place we met and fell in love."

Rory hugged her to his side. "I like the way you think."

"Anita," Saber called.

London stood at Saber's side and bore a smug grin.

"You can go home. London and I can take care of Rory's people. Will that be okay, Rory?"

"Aye," he said.

"We'll do a quick tour of Middlemarch before I take you to my place. Do you have suitcases?" she asked.

"Henry and Gerard are delivering the luggage. Henry told me he'd leave yours at the door," Saber said.

"Coming, Toby?" Anita asked, holding out her hand.

The small boy didn't hesitate to take her hand. Rory took her other, and she led the pair to her vehicle. She smiled wide, almost breathless with positivity and joy. "Let's go home."

"You told me Middlemarch was beautiful," Rory murmured as they sat in front of the fire.

Toby was safely in bed and seemed settled. He didn't let his lack of an arm stop him, but Rory had told her it had been difficult at first, and Toby missed his parents. Sometimes, he woke with nightmares.

Anita wished she could kill Elizabeth Henderson herself. Even though she understood Rory would blame himself, he must appreciate, at some level, that he'd needed to act for himself and the pack.

"Thank you for giving me a second chance and for welcoming Toby into your life," Rory said. "I know the second part is a lot to ask, but I feel responsible. My grandmother—"

"You don't have to explain. Toby's presence makes me love you more. It proves you have an enormous heart and care for the people under your protection. It gives me confidence you'll fit in here in Middlemarch, and even better, you'll make me the best of mates."

Rory's expression softened. "I love you, Anita, and I apologize for the suffering inflicted on you because of my grandmother. It's clear now the felines broke something inside her when they massacred her family. It's not an excuse, but it explains her abominable behavior."

"You feel guilty."

"I should've noticed the rot in my pack."

"Didn't your people have complaints?"

"Nay, but they should've felt they could talk to me. My grandmother was careful. My best friend, Marcus, was unaware of the problems because he would've told me the truth."

"Did Marcus come with you to Middlemarch?"

"Aye, but I don't want to speak about Marcus or my grandmother or anything else."

Her brows arched. "What would you like to discuss?"

"Us. Our future." He stood and pulled a small black box from his trouser pocket. "I love you, Anita. I might've taken time to reach this conclusion, but my wolf and I want you. Your feline. We want you in our future. We wish to savor the good and help to shoulder the burdens that come along. Will you please marry me and be my forever mate?" He opened the box, but his gaze remained on her.

Breathlessness gripped her, and she gasped in air while her smile started slowly and turned toothy. She stared at the sparkling ring, which was a blend of diamonds and sapphires. The sapphires reminded her of his eyes.

"Anita?"

"Yes." She flew into Rory's arms, their lips met, and everything was perfect.

Rory pulled back. "Let me see the ring on your finger." He took her left hand and tugged the ring from the box. He slipped it over her knuckle and smiled with satisfaction. "Perfect."

She curled her fingers around his and stooped to grab the TV remote. After turning the telly off, she tugged him from the lounge, only pausing to switch off the light.

They stopped at Toby's room and checked on him. He lay in the middle of the bed, letting out tiny snores. Anita grinned, part of her glad she had a second chance to raise a child. Her gut told her Toby's presence would strengthen them, and they'd blend into a beautiful family.

In her bedroom—their bedroom now—Anita toed off her shoes and removed her clothes while watching Rory.

"Sweetheart, I love your beautiful mind." He grinned and stripped faster than her. She was still wearing a pair of lacy white panties when he lifted her off her feet. Seconds later, the mattress was at her back, and she smiled up at him, her heart so full she feared it might burst.

Desire flared hotter as their lips met, and her feline released a loud purr of contentment. Rory chuckled against her mouth and took the kiss deeper. Passion exploded, and her heart thundered because each of his touches fueled her desire. Now that she'd stopped fighting, the physical contact sent magic soaring through her, and the sense of rightness was off the charts.

"Rory, I love you. My enthusiasm about my trip to Scotland fooled everyone, but inside I was miserable. I thought... I thought I'd lost you again, and it was killing me inside. Seeing you here is like a dream."

"Once I contacted Saber, everything traveled at speed. He made me think I was doing the right thing."

"Absolutely," Anita said. "Your people need to heal. A fresh start will help. You have your woodworking skills, which will mean more job opportunities for locals. I assume you're going to start up your business?"

"Aye, but no more talking. We can do that later," Rory promised, stealing a quick kiss. He ran his finger over the band of the ring he'd given her earlier and offered her a satisfied smile. "Right now, I want to love you, and if you're willing, I'd like to mark you, so every other shifter male understands you're mine."

"That works both ways."

"Exactly, and I'll wear your mark with pride."

Anita laughed, her happiness and joy spilling free. She shoved at his shoulder, and he let her roll him. Immediately, she claimed the top position and explored his muscular body. While she kissed and stroked, he traced the band of her panties, gave a sharp jerk, and tugged them free.

"My first purchase will be a set of lingerie for my beautiful mate."

She wagged her finger. "Don't think I won't hold you to that."

"Too much talk. Not enough action," Rory reminded her with a cheeky smile.

She ran her fingers over his shoulders and lowered her body to drag her nipples across his chest.

"My turn," he said, seconds before he reclaimed the top spot.

He caged her in his arms and started his romantic assault on her mouth. The lazy stroke of his tongue against hers only drove the tension between them higher. Their lips clung, and she was soon drowning in desire.

"You feel amazing," he whispered. "I doubt I'll ever tire of touching you, tasting you."

Anita understood what he meant. Like perfect puzzle pieces, they fit. Things became more serious, the touches lingering and sweet. With his knee, he parted her legs. Rory ran his finger along her slit and tested her readiness.

"Please don't make me wait," she whispered.

Rory rose over her and pushed home in one sweet thrust. "I'm impatient too. Hungry for what I've been missing."

He pulled one nipple into his mouth, giving her hot, tight suction that reverberated straight to her pussy. She groaned and clung to him. Anita kissed his shoulder, and he stretched his neck to allow her to nip him at the marking site.

His groan filled her with ferocious heat and drove her to bite down harder. When Rory copied her actions, his hips flexing as he thrust and withdrew in achingly slow increments, she couldn't prevent another groan of pleasure. His teeth scored the fleshy pad at the juncture of neck and shoulder.

Anita growled, and her sharp teeth pierced his flesh, drawing blood. A whip of pain followed Rory's bite, but before she could process the level of it, the discomfort morphed to acute pleasure. She whimpered, instinct telling her not to release Rory yet.

His hips shifted, and somehow, he kept up his thrusts.

"Touch yourself, lass."

She comprehended his garbled words and followed his instructions, strumming her clit. She toppled into her climax at the next stroke. One sweep of her finger had her coming apart and whimpers she couldn't contain escaped.

With blissful pleasure sweeping through her, she released her teeth and licked the wound she'd inflicted. Rory lifted his head and groaned, so she repeated the move with a swish of her tongue. His roar of pleasure echoed through the bedroom. He drove into her and stilled, balls deep, his cock pulsing as he came. Long seconds later, he cleaned the mark he'd bestowed on her, and she understood.

That one lick shoved a wash of intense enjoyment in her, and a spasm tore through her. She felt a tightening and realized Rory had buried deep and knotted with her.

"Well, lass. Our animals accept each other."

"Is this normal with wolves?"

"Nay," Rory said. "This has only ever happened with you, so I'm assuming it's because we're mates."

"Oh. What do you suppose the purpose is?"

"I'm thinking it's to do with making babies."

"But I take a birth control shot."

Rory laughed. "Would you mind if you became pregnant?"

"No," she said after thinking about it for a brief second. "I couldn't think of a better way to celebrate."

"I agree, but I don't mind waiting, either. We should settle into a routine first, especially since we have Toby. Thank you for accepting him. I don't know what I would've done if you'd objected."

"Never gonna happen. I know what rejection is like, and if anyone deserves a happy ending, it's this wee boy. He's been through enough."

Rory sobered. "I agree. I love you, lass. Your bravery and courage have shown me the way forward, and now I've found you, I'm excited about the adventures we'll have together."

"Me too," Anita said. "Thank you for coming to find me."

"I missed you from the moment we parted. My wolf and I were miserable without you."

"Right back at you." Anita reached up to kiss him, their embrace tender and full of love. Then he wrapped her in his arms, and they made love again. Slow. Consuming. *Forever.*

Chapter 25

Epilogue

"This is so much fun," Rory said. "We should've done this in Scotland. Maybe the pack wouldn't have imploded if we'd built closer bonds."

Anita ran her hand over his stubbled chin. "It wasn't entirely your fault. Deep down, you know that."

"I do," he said. "But innocent wolves suffered because I was slow to understand what was happening under my nose."

"You've helped the wolves who came with you—the ones who trusted you enough to start a life in Middlemarch—and the community. Oh, it looks as if we're about to start our run. Do you think Toby will keep up?"

"If he tires, I don't mind hanging back," Rory said. "Middlemarch has been good for him, and the kids have accepted him without the teasing I expected."

"He told Tomasine's boys his father used to beat him. It seems he was concerned Felix might punish Bryce and Liam for a little prank they played. Tomasine told me," Anita said.

"We haven't struck Toby."

"No," she said. "But it appears Toby has nightmares about doing the wrong thing by mistake."

"He thinks we might reject him," Rory guessed.

"Yes."

Rory stood and hauled Anita to her feet. "We'll talk to him together. Tell him he's stuck with us. If we ever get angry at something he has done, his punishment will be the loss of a treat, not a physical beating."

"Sounds like a plan."

A whistle blew, and the assembled shifters quietened. An elderly feline man spoke. "Just a couple of warnings. Please keep the howls or roaring down until we're deep in the mountains. Saber will lead, and he'll let you know when it's okay to vocalize. Care for each other, and keep an eye on the youngsters. Other than that, enjoy the run. Go ahead and get ready."

"Toby," Anita called.

Toby raced over to her. "Anita," he said. "Bryce and Liam can't shift like me."

"That's right," she said. "I didn't have my first shift until I turned thirteen. Feline shifters don't shift as early as wolves, so you're lucky. Are you looking forward to the run?"

"I wish Liam and Bryce could run too," Toby said.

"We'll see them later at the café," Rory said. "You can tell them about your run, then."

He brightened at hearing this, his attention wandering back to the various pack members.

"Toby, have you met Kian?" Anita asked. "You're around the same age. He's a snow leopard."

Toby shot her an interested look. "Kian?"

Anita scanned the crowd. "Both of you come with me, and I'll introduce you to Kian and his parents. Hey, Isabella. Leo," she said. "You haven't met my mate, Rory, or our foster son, Toby."

"Pleased to meet you," Leo said, extending his hand. "Saber told me you were coming to live in Middlemarch. Welcome."

While Rory chatted with Leo and Isabella, Anita monitored Toby and Kian.

"You shift?" Toby asked Kian.

Kian nodded.

"Kian, can you run with Toby and show him what to do?" Leo asked, obviously watching the kids, too.

"Yes," Kian said, his blond head bobbing.

It surprised Anita that Kian didn't ask about Toby's missing arm, but perhaps Leo or Isabella had explained this to Kian earlier.

A whistle blew again, and silence fell among the crowd. Saber stood on a rock and spoke to the group. "Thank you for coming. Our run gets bigger every time, and the Feline Council loves the enthusiasm of these evening runs. A few reminders—look after our youngsters. Watch out for humans. Henry is training his dogs, so we have a ready excuse for any unexplained sightings but still watch for the unexpected. We're meeting at the pub for drinks, or those with children might prefer ice cream or coffee or an early dinner at the café. Both places will be open. I'll lead off in a moment. Please leave in groups of five. A cat clan or a pack of wolves will attract attention, which we do not want. Have fun."

Anita helped Toby undress—more so she could keep track of his clothes.

"Would you like to run with us?" Isabella asked, her smile friendly. "It might be good for the boys. We're doing a shorter version then heading to the café."

Anita shared a glance with Rory, and he nodded. "Sounds perfect," she said.

Five minutes later, they were on their way. Toby scampered along on three legs, taking the hill without pause. Kian ran at his side, keeping pace, and Anita smiled because it was apparent the young snow leopard could go faster. He didn't, and warmth filled Anita. She wasn't sure why she'd been so worried about Rory fitting into her Middlemarch life.

The hilly loop took them an hour to run. Their group paused at the high point to appreciate the view. Great gray schist piles showed amongst the light snow coating on the slope below, and the river flowed farther down in the valley, cutting its way through the land. The town nestled even farther away, and already lights burned through windows and fought the approaching night.

Leo barked out a command and set off. Kian and Toby followed him down a different path, trailed by Isabella. Rory waited a fraction longer, and when Anita gave a low call of enquiry, he nuzzled her flank. A wealth of love filled her heart, and she shifted body positions to rub her nose against his. Then they trotted after the boys, Leo and Isabella.

Back at the car, they shifted and dressed before driving to town. Their vehicle was much noisier on the homeward trip since Kian sat in the rear seat with Toby, the pair chattering about their run, Toby's lack of an arm, and which ice cream they might have at the café. It was so ordinary she smiled.

"I love you, Anita," Rory said in a low voice as he drove toward Middlemarch.

She turned to him, surprised by his intensity. "I know," she said simply.

"Thanks to you, the wolves who matter to me have a fresh start. If I hadn't met you at the gathering, I don't know what might've happened."

"I like to think fate put us back on the right path," she said.

"The residents here are happy, and there's a quiet satisfaction in the air with none of the silent tension I used to wonder about at Castle Henderson. My wolves are relaxed and purposeful, and Toby is settling nicely. I want you to know I appreciate you, and I can't believe how right it feels with you at my side."

Anita smiled, pleasure filling her at his words. The rejection so long ago might've changed the course of her life, but they'd gone full circle, and she'd never felt happier. The loneliness had faded, and her days were full of friendship and love and togetherness.

"I think," she drawled with a mischievous wink at her mate, "that throwing up on a man grabs their attention."

Rory barked out a laugh and parked the SUV outside the café. "Lass, that might be one of the most original ways of attracting notice. I was more bemused than upset, even though it was my favorite kilt. One look at you, and I knew my life would never be the same. You've given us friends and family and a place to call home."

Anita's phone beeped with an incoming text. "Should we continue this conversation later tonight in privacy?"

"That'd work for me," Rory said with a grin.

Anita glanced at her phone. "It's a text from Ramsay," she said.

"What does it say?"

"**Don't believe anything you read in the papers. I'm innocent**," Anita read. "What do you suppose that means?"

"You know Ramsay better than me." Rory climbed out of the vehicle and helped the boys exit.

The boys ran into the café with Kian leading the way. She gave Rory a quick hug and tucked her phone away. "I'll call him tomorrow."

Rory took Anita's hand, and they followed the boys, the welcoming call of friends greeting them when they stepped inside the café.

They were home.

Wondering what is up with Ramsay?
The last time we saw Anita's friend, Ramsay, he was in the pub. If you're curious about what happened to him, check out his story in *My Highland Fling*.

Afterword

I hope you loved the first book in the Middlemarch Shifters spinoff series, **Middlemarch Gathering**. If you did, please feel free to leave an enthusiastic review for *MY HIGHLAND MATE* and rave about my brilliance at your favored online bookstore. *grin*

Don't want to miss a new book? Sign up for my entertaining newsletter at www.shelleymunro.com/newsletter.

Thanks for reading!
Shelley

About Author

USA Today bestselling author Shelley Munro lives in Auckland, the City of Sails, with her husband and a cheeky Jack Russell/mystery breed dog.

Typical New Zealanders, Shelley and her husband left home for their big OE soon after they married (translation of New Zealand speak - big overseas experience). A twelve-month-long adventure lengthened to six years of roaming the world. Enduring memories include being almost sat on by a mountain gorilla in Rwanda, lazing on white sandy beaches in India, whale watching in Alaska, searching for leprechauns in Ireland, and dealing with ghosts in an English pub.

While travel is still a big attraction, these days Shelley is most likely found in front of her computer following another love - that of writing stories of contemporary and paranormal romance and adventure. Other interests include watching rugby (strictly for research purposes), cycling, playing croquet and the ukelele, and curling up with an enjoyable book. Visit Shelley at her website www. shelleymunro.com.

Also By Shelley

Middlemarch Gathering
My Highland Mate
My Highland Fling

Middlemarch Capture
Snared by Saber
Favored by Felix
Lost with Leo
Spellbound with Sly
Journey with Joe
Star-Crossed with Scarlett

Lightning Source UK Ltd.
Milton Keynes UK
UKHW040652190722
406066UK00002B/438